BEVERLY HILLS PUBLIC LIBRARY   DUPL

3 5048 00812 4909

WITHDRAWN

D1006683

J
FICTION
Hathaway

letters to missy violet

BY BARBARA HATHAWAY

Houghton Mifflin
Houghton Mifflin Harcourt
Boston   New York   2012

Beverly Hills Public Library
WITHDRAWN
Beverly Hills, California 90210

This book is dedicated to my first cousins,
Mary Alice Bishop and Lyman Brandon,
and to the memory of their mother,
Cornelia Davis.

Copyright © 2012 by Barbara Hathaway

All rights reserved. For information about permission to reproduce selections from this book, write to Permissions, Houghton Mifflin Harcourt Publishing Company, 215 Park Avenue South, New York, New York 10003.

Houghton Mifflin is an imprint of Houghton Mifflin Harcourt Publishing Company.

www.hmhbooks.com

The text of this book is set in Granjon.

Library of Congress Cataloging-in-Publication Data
Hathaway, Barbara, 1944–
Letters to Missy Violet / by Barbara Hathaway.
p. cm.
Summary: While her friend Missy Violet, the town midwife, is away in Florida, eleven-year-old Viney concerns herself with ailing neighbors, schoolmates, and her irrepressible cousin Charles, who feels superior because he has been to Harlem in New York City.
ISBN 978-0-547-36300-4
1. African Americans—Juvenile fiction. [1. African Americans—Fiction.
2. Letters—Fiction. 3. Southern States—History—1865–1951—Fiction.] I. Title.
PZ7.H2819Le 2012
[Fic]—dc23
2011012162

Manufactured in the United States of America.
DOC 10 9 8 7 6 5 4 3 2 1

4500332149

A New Teacher

It is August and school has already started. We have a new teacher, Miss Glover. She's nice-looking, brown and smooth like peanut butter, and wears her hair pulled back in a bun. She's not loud and bossy like Miss Battle, our old teacher. Miss Battle is mean and yelps like a yard dog. She makes you learn, though.

Miss Glover makes you learn, too, but she makes learning fun. She brings in lots of pictures and maps and books for us to look at. She'll even let you take some of them home if you promise to take good care of them and bring them back. A lot of the pictures are of places she's been to. And if she makes you read in front of the class and you miss a word or say it wrong or something, she won't shame you in front of everybody. She'll just call you up to her desk and help you with the words you said wrong. And no one else can hear what she says to you but you and her.

Another thing Miss Glover doesn't do: She won't give you a licking with the ruler. Miss Battle will give you a licking right in front of the whole class and then go tell your folks you been acting up in school. She'll even tell your grandma and your grandpa when she sees them in church on Sunday. Miss Glover would never do that—she believes children should be talked to. If any switching needs to be done, she says it ought to be done at home. She's always having to talk to my cousin Charles. Sometimes I think he cuts up just so Miss Glover will take him to the back of the room and talk to him. You should see his face when he's getting talked to—his eyes get all dreamy-looking and he grins like a Cheshire cat.

Charles sits next to a real pretty girl named Winsome Blue. He's sweet on Winsome but he doesn't want my friend Arma Jean Pettegrue to know, because he's sweet on Arma Jean, too. He doesn't know how to act when both of them are in the same place at the same time. When

Winsome is around he gets all silly and clumsy and starts dropping things on the floor. But when Arma Jean is around he gets all mannish and acts all biggity, strutting and talking that Harlem talk he learned while he was up in New York City this summer, like "Gimme some skin, man!" and "Dig that crazy jive!" I sure hate that he had to come back down here to Richmond County to go to school again this year. I wish his poor mama would get well so he could go back home.

But getting back to Miss Glover, most of the parents just love her and they all gather around her at church, except for Mister Waters, Cleveland Waters's daddy. Mister Waters says his boy don't need "all that book learnin' and coddlin'" Miss Glover trying to do. He asked Miss Glover, "What Cleveland need with so much book learnin' when the South ain't gonna let him be nothin' but a sharecropper?" He even comes to school and plucks Cleveland right out of the class whenever he wants him to work in the field. Too bad, because Cleveland likes school and catches on real quick, especially to things that have to do with numbers.

Miss Glover tried to talk to Mister Waters one day when he came to take Cleveland out of class. She spoke real nice to him but he got all loud and talked to her rough like he was trying to scare her. Told her she was "fillin' the children's heads with foolish notions, talkin' to them 'bout travelin' and such." Then he said something that made all of us children feel ashamed. He asked Miss Glover if she really believed any of us colored children would grow up to be anything other than somebody's maid or farm hand. Miss Glover stood back and looked him straight in the eye and said, "My dear Mister Waters, you are looking at a colored child who grew up to be something other than a maid or a farm hand!" And Mister Waters couldn't say a word. But he took Cleveland out of the class anyway.

After they left, Miss Glover reminded us that there was nothing wrong with being a maid or a farm hand as long as you were honest and hard working. She said, "Education and good morals will lift the colored people up." I hope we keep Miss Glover forever!

MISS ROULA OLETTE

Just before school started Missy Violet had to go down to Tallahassee, Florida, to see about her sick brother, but she gave me his address and told me it was fine for me to write. Missy Violet and I are very good friends now. She says I'm her best helper girl because I helped her "catch babies" this summer. But Mama told me not to bother Missy Violet with letters while she was down in Tallahassee. Mama said, "Don't go tantalizin' the life out of Missy Violet with a lot of letters, worryin' her about things goin' on up here at home. She got enough on her mind takin' care of a sick brother." And she shook her finger at me.

I told Mama that Missy Violet was expecting me to write and tell her all about school but Mama said, "No!" So I had to sneak and write a letter. I hated to disobey Mama, but I just had to tell Missy Violet about Miss Roula Olette! Miss Roula is Missy Violet's good friend and she is in a bad way. So I borrowed an envelope and a stamp from my big sister Savannah's stationery box and wrote the letter on a piece of paper I tore out of my composition book. I hope Savannah won't miss her envelope and her stamp. Now all I have to do is get the letter down to the post office window at the general store before Mama finds out about it.

August 14, 1929
Dear Missy Violet,

I just had to write and tell you about poor Miss Roula. I think she is gone sick in the head. She won't eat anything except oatmeal and squash and goes wandering around in the cemetery in her housecoat! I think she's acting that way because her snooty ol' daughter Amabelle came down here from New York City and made her

stop taking the boneset tonic you gave her
for her tired blood and poor circulation.
I know Miss Roula has some because you
sent Charles and me over to her house with
a great big jar full before you went away.
Mama told her daughter about the tonic
but Amabelle claims she can't find it.

Missy Violet, I don't like Amabelle one
bit. She looks at people down the side
of her nose like she thinks she's superior.
Charles doesn't like her either—he calls
her "astorperious." That's a word he picked
up up in Harlem this summer. He says
it means "stuck up." Something about
Amabelle reminds me of my classmate
Margie Poole. I bet Margie will be just
like her when she grows up, all snooty and
superior-acting. Both of them are know-it-
alls. I won't forget how Margie laughed at
me because I thought babies came out of a
tree stump.

I can tell Amabelle thinks she's good-
looking, and she does have all that pretty

black hair hanging down her back, but to me she's not as pretty as Miss Roula is. She looks like an ol' yellow pumpkin to me. She's talking about taking Miss Roula back up north with her to live. Poor Miss Roula doesn't know anybody up north. Amabelle hardly lets her have visitors now. Like the other day when Mister Johnnie Browne stopped by to see how Miss Roula was doing, Amabelle looked him up and down, wrinkled her nose, and said, "You need to do somethin' about that rash all over your face and arms before you go visitin' folks." Hurt Mister Johnnie's feelings something awful. He came over to the house with water in his eyes, telling Mama and Papa about what happened.

Charles says he's gonna put a cow patty in Amabelle's car. I hope he does.

Missy Violet, I also have some good news. We have a new teacher at school. Her name is Miss Glover and she is a fine teacher. I look forward to going to school every day now. Even Charles gets up and gets ready in the morning without giving Mama any trouble. You will like Miss Glover because she encourages us to read. You always do that, Missy Violet. You always say, "Read, children, read!" Well, we are doing lots of reading now. Miss Glover brings the newspaper to class every day and we all have to take turns reading from it. Maybe you will get to meet her when you come home. She attends church every third Sunday.

That's all for now, except that the ax handle fell on Papa's foot while he was working in the woodshed and now Mama's making him stay off it. When it happened I was at home and ran with Mama to the woodshed when Papa hollered for help. When I saw how his foot was bleeding I remembered what you taught me about bloody wounds and told Mama not to wipe the blood off, but to tie it up in its own blood because that would start the healing right away. Later, when we got Papa back to the house, Mama cleaned the wound and bandaged it up. And we put cayenne liniment on it every day just the way you did for Mister Cook when he cut his foot on the tractor. Papa and Mama were surprised that I knew how to make cayenne liniment and how to take care of wounds. I was glad I remembered what you had taught me.

Papa is complaining about having to stay put all the time, but he makes sure that one of the boys goes down to your house every day to feed your dog, Duke, and milk the cow.

Please write to me and tell me what to do about Miss Roula, and say hello to your brother for me.

I sure wish we could find that boneset tonic.

From your best helper girl,

Viney

A Letter from Missy Violet

Uh-oh! Mama found out I wrote to Missy Violet. The letter came on a Saturday. Usually Savannah or one of the boys takes in the mail on Saturday, but that Saturday Mama brought in the mail. "Look, Viney, here's a letter for you from Missy Violet," she said with a smile on her face.

Both of my ears started to ring. I didn't want Mama to see that letter. I snatched the letter out of Mama's hand and tried to walk away real fast. I shouldn't have done that, because Mama is as quick as a rattlesnake. She snatched the letter right back, her smile turned to a frown.

"You wrote to Missy Violet and told her about Miss Roula, didn't you," Mama said in that voice she uses when one of us kids does something she doesn't like behind her back. Then she made me go into the parlor and read the letter out loud in front of her and Papa.

August 25, 1929

Dear Viney,

Hope this letter finds you and the family doing fine. Brother is coming along slowly, but I pray that with God's help, he will be back on his feet soon. It was so good to hear from you, Viney. Your penmanship is very neat; it is a pleasure to read.

So you met Amabelle. I know her very well, from the day she was born. You see, I attended her birth — that's how long her mother and I have been friends. I'm sorry you don't like her, but she is not so bad. She doesn't think she is superior. She just likes things done a certain way. She has always been like that. She's particular, that's all. Even when she was a little girl she was very neat and careful with her things. She is the same way about her mama. She really is a good daughter, and I believe if she could find the boneset tonic she would give it to Roula.

Tell her to look underneath the bed. Roula has been hiding things under the bed for quite some time now. I'm afraid my dear friend is getting a little feeble-minded. I believe the tonic will help her, but don't expect her to be like she was before. I believe something happened to her mind when her husband passed away. But don't worry, Viney. Miss Roula will be fine up in New York with her daughter. Amabelle will see that she gets good care.

You are a sweet child, Viney, to worry so much about other people. That is why I think you would make a good midwife.

I'm so happy to hear about your new teacher. I think I got a glimpse of her at church one Sunday. She is pretty, in a quiet, dainty way. Sorry I didn't get to meet her. I'm so happy she encourages you children to read. If you know how to read well you can learn most anything.

Give a special hello to my redheaded boy,

Charles. You and Charles are my special dumplings. Tell him not to put a cow patty in Amabelle's car — that wouldn't be nice. Remember, you reap what you sow. Tell him to write me and let me know how he is doing in school, too. Be good to one another.

Give all the family my love. Tell your daddy to stay off that foot as much as he can. And I'm so proud that you remembered what I taught you about bleeding wounds. Good job! Thank your daddy and all the children for looking after Duke and the cow for me. Hope to hear from you again soon. Be a good girl — study hard and say your prayers.

Yours very truly,

Missy Violet

After I read the letter, Mama told Papa she was going to whup me for being so fast and nosin' in grown folks' business. I think Papa was tickled, but Mama didn't think it was funny at all! Mama took the letter from me and kept shaking it at me. "Viney Eleanor, didn't I tell you not to go worryin' Missy Violet with letters and things while she's down there in Tallahassee?" she said. She never calls me Viney Eleanor unless she's real mad.

I wish she had taken me aside like Miss Glover would have done instead of talking all in front of Charles. He loves to see people get into trouble. I saw a big smirk sneak across his face when Mama chastised me, and I could hear him laughing underneath his breath until Mama saw him and reminded him about the part of the letter that told about the cow patty. That wiped the grin off his face right quick. I tried to explain to him later that I was really on his side about the cow patty, but he wouldn't speak to me. "I'll getcha for this!" was all he said.

Mama made me go in the yard and get her a switch. Then she made me go to her room and sit on the bed until she was ready to whup me. But before she came in the room she fussed about the letter all afternoon and poor Papa had to sit and listen because he couldn't walk away on his sore foot. I kept poking my head out of the bedroom door to let Papa know he wasn't the only one in misery, that I was miserable waiting in the bedroom too.

"I can't believe that gal went behind my back and wrote that letter!" Mama kept saying. "I didn't know that child had such Judas ways." That really hurt my feelings when Mama called me Judas. I hate for Mama or Papa to be mad at me. Nothing feels right until they get glad again. "I'm gonna fix her business good with that switch!" Mama kept saying. "Goin' behind my back writin' that letter, sayin' all those awful things about Amabelle. Amabelle is a good woman. I'll never forget how she helped me when my grandmama was sick. She'd come by every day and give me a hand. Ooooh, I'm gonna get that Viney real good with that switch. You'll see."

Then I heard Papa say, "Amabelle is kind of persnickety, Lena." I think Papa was trying to help me out.

"I know she a handful," Mama said. "But Viney had no right talkin' that way about a grown woman and tellin' Miss Roula's business like that."

"The child didn't mean no harm, Lena," Papa said. "She just worried 'bout Miss Roula. I think it's kinda sweet. Besides, she didn't say nothin' that wasn't true. It does seem like Miss Roula done gone around the bend. Roamin' up there in the cemetery in her housecoat."

"I know," said Mama. "She's probably up there lookin'

for her husband's grave. She probably forgot where he's buried."

"How long were they married?" Papa asked.

"About thirty-eight or forty years, I reckon," Mama answered.

"Treated Miss Roula like a china doll," Mama told Papa. "She was never the same after he passed away, poor soul. Her heart was just eaten up with grief. I reckon I'd feel the same way if anything ever happened to you, James," Mama said, and her voice sounded all funny and cracked.

"Honey, you would miss me that much?" Papa asked.

"Sho' I would," Mama answered.

"Come here," Papa said, and I stuck my head out the bedroom door. And there was Mama and Papa sitting together on the settee with their arms locked around each other. I put my hands over my mouth so they wouldn't hear me giggle.

"I'll go over to Miss Roula's tomorrow and tell Amabelle to look underneath the bed for the jar of boneset tonic," Mama said.

Later on Mama came and sat down next to me on her bed and explained to me about Miss Roula. She said that sometimes when people start to get old, their mind starts to go. It starts to play tricks on them and they may say and do foolish things. "That's the way life is sometimes, honey. And we just have to accept it," Mama said. She didn't give me the whupping she promised me, and she said I could write to Missy Violet, but only about school.

Charles and Missy Violet
Write to Each Other

August 28, 1929

Hey Missy Violet, this here is Charles,

    I diding write you befor now becose Viney didn't tell me you sed to write. I jus snucked up on her reading a letter you rote her one day and then she tell me you say to write. She always keeping things lak that to hersef like she grown or somethin. Then when she give me the address she say "Don't be worryin Missy Violet wit a whole lotta letters." But I ain't payin her no mind. She just gellous becose I went to New York City.

She say, "Charles, don't you know nothing els to talk about besides New York City?"

I'm gonna write about my trip in the essay contess. I know its gonna be good and I am gonna win firs prise, cose I seen everything up in New York Ciy folks down here ain't never seen! All kinds of cars and peoples. I saw Buicks and Cadillacs and Oldsmobiles. Even big ol Packards like Mister Som Grit got. I even saw Mayor Jimmy Walker ridin around in his Duesenberg. Diding see no old timey cars on the streets up there.

I even rode downtown on the subway, that's a cho cho train that runs under the ground. I was just lookin and lookin all around. Downtown I saw all the tall billdins and stores where the rich people shops. But they got plenty stores up in Harlem too.

A lotta people up in Harlem got radios. They lissen to the ball game and the boxin match and music and evything! They lissen to the Amos and Andy Show. A show about

colard people livin in Harlem. Bess show I
ever heard. Wish we had it down here. "Ow
wah, ow wah, ow wah!" That's what Amos and
Andy say at the end of the show. Don't none
of the colard people down here have radios.
I asked Mama and Papa about getting one.
Papa sed they cos too much money and use up
too much lectricity. Mama sed it was the
work of the devil and wood catch the house on
fire when it thunderstorms. She say she even
hear people say they wood make you sick. Papa
say he not even sure they have the Amos and
Andy show down here. Everybody down here all
wet, man. When I gets grown, I'm gonna buy
mysef a Buick and drive back up to New York
City quic as I can. Man, I love that Big
Apple!

  Missy Violet, when you comin home? I am
tired of Viney ackin like you lef her boss
over evything. Bring me something from
Floreda when you come back.

  Charles

September 9, 1929

Dear Charles,

   How is my handsome redheaded boy! Missy Violet was so glad to hear from you. I'm happy you had such a good time up in New York City. I have never been there, though I hear it is some fine place. I would love to see Harlem, a place with lots of different kinds of colored people all living together. Maybe someday before I get too old I'll get a chance to visit. Maybe you will drive me up there in your Buick when you finish school?

   I think it's nice you want to go back when you grow up, but, child, you must go back with some schooling under your cap. Please try to finish school. You know the world is changing all the time and there is a place for colored in every trade.

   Charles, I enjoyed your letter so much, but I want you to work on your spelling, son. I know you can do this because you spelled the names of all those cars you liked correctly. I think if you take your time and learn to spell the small everyday words well, you will have a good chance of winning that contest.

How is your dear mama? Is she feeling better? I pray so. Give her and your papa my regards when you see them. I am sorry they would not let you have a radio — I would love to have one myself. But they are expensive, costing between fifty and one hundred dollars, I've heard. I don't know how so many people in Harlem can afford one. Maybe they buy on time or maybe they buy used radios. Whatever it is, it certainly would be nice to have one. I guess one day we all will.

Charles, I just love it when you children write to me. You and Viney are my special dumplings. I miss you both and look forward to seeing you all when I get back home. Be good in school — mind the teacher and work hard at your lessons. And remember to say your prayers.

Yours very truly,
Missy Violet

SPECIAL CARE

September 11, 1929
Dear Missy Violet,

  I have some bad news: Not long after
school got started, our favorite teacher,
Miss Glover, got married and moved away!
She married a man from Fayetteville. That's
all we know about him. He came to church
one Sunday, but nobody knew who he was.
And nobody knew he was there looking for
Miss Glover. Well, nobody except Arma
Jean, that is. She figured it out right

away. While we were walking on the church grounds that morning she said, "Look at that fine-lookin' man. I bet he got his cap set for Miss Glover." Yep, that's what she said, just like that! Arma Jean's good at figuring things out. She figured out that Charles was sweet on Winsome, too.

More bad news: Miss Battle is back! And the first thing she did was change our desk partners. She made me sit next to Margie Poole even though she knows I've been sitting next to Arma Jean ever since the first grade. I hate sitting next to Margie Poole—she acts so uppity and snooty. I try to be nice to her but she acts like I'm not even there. I sure miss sitting next to Arma Jean and she misses sitting next to me, too. All we can do now is wave and give each other sad smiles from across the room. Sometimes, Arma Jean mouths me a silent message. I can read her lips real good. She mouths, "See you at recess," or "What you got for lunch?" Sometimes she

gets caught and Miss Battle scolds her.
"YOUNG LADY!" she shouts. "IF YOU TALK
ACROSS THE ROOM ONE MORE TIME,
YOU'LL GO STAND IN THE CORNER!"
Then everybody looks at Arma Jean, and
Arma Jean snaps her head back around to
the front. That's when Margie Poole just
smirks and looks all satisfied and I want to
hit her in the head with a brick.

Arma Jean now sits next to a big ol',
simple-lookin' girl named Ruby Dean Baker.
Ruby Dean should be sitting in the back
with the older children, but Miss Battle
says Ruby Dean is slow and puts her in the
middle with the eleven- and twelve-year-
olds. Miss Glover wouldn't have done that.
All the kids tease Ruby Dean about sitting
with the younger children because she is so
big, but I try not to join in because Mama
says, "Do unto others as you would have
them do unto you." And I sure wouldn't
like to have all those kids teasing me.

But Ruby Dean is pretty slow. Even Miss Battle can't make her learn.

Missy Violet, you would say that Ruby Dean needs "special care." The kind of care you give to little babies who won't nurse or who are slow to grow. I remember one time I went with you to catch a baby named William—"Teeny William" you called him because he was so small.

You looked worried when you saw how little he was. You didn't think he was going to live. Right away you grabbed three baby blankets and laid them one on top of the other and wrapped Teeny William up in them real tight. Then you warmed a brick in the fireplace and wrapped it in a cloth and put it underneath his cradle. "We got to keep this baby warm, warm, warm," you told his mama and his papa.

But poor Teeny William wouldn't nurse, so you went by his house every day and showed his mother how to feed him with an eyedropper. William still wouldn't take his mother's milk, remember? You said this happens sometimes with sickly babies—the mother's milk is too rich for the sick baby's stomach. So you brought soybean milk to the house and mixed it with a little water and squeezed it into Teeny William's mouth with the eyedropper and Teeny William kept it down.

Every day you would go by to see how Teeny William was doing and once a week you would weigh him on your funny little scale. Soon Teeny William started to nurse and to pick up weight. Now he is four months old and plump as an apple dumpling! I think that's the kind of special care Miss Glover would give Ruby Dean if she had stayed, because you and Miss Glover are kind ladies.

I think Miss Glover had already started to give Ruby Dean special care, because she would give her things to do like collecting papers and passing out books. Ruby Dean did a good job, too, and Miss Glover praised her in front of the whole class.

Miss Battle just says, "Ruby Dean, there's nothing wrong with you. You're just lazy." She makes Ruby Dean go up to the blackboard to do arithmetic. Ruby Dean is afraid of arithmetic the way most people are afraid of snakes. And when she walks up to the front the floor boards creak and the kids laugh. Then poor Ruby just stands there in front of the board scratching her head and rocking from side to side. Then Miss Battle says, "Ruby, this lesson is not that hard—even the first-graders can do it." Then she scolds her for rocking. "Stop that rocking, child. You're not a boat!" she hollers, and the children laugh some more.

When I tell Mama how bad Miss Battle treats Ruby Dean, she says Miss Battle is just trying to get her to learn. But Mama did say she could do it in a more Christian way.

One week, Miss Battle didn't get a

chance to pick on Ruby Dean at all because she had her hands full with a little girl named Nettie. Nettie had never been to school before and every day when her papa dropped her off she would cry and cry and cry. Nothing Miss Battle said or did made her stop crying.

Miss Battle made her stand in the corner and promised to give her a licking, but even that didn't do any good. Nettie just hollered louder. But then a funny thing happened one day: Nettie was crying and Ruby Dean got up from her seat and went over and put her arm around the little girl's shoulder and talked to her in a real soft voice and the little girl stopped crying. She lay in Ruby Dean's arms like Ruby Dean was her mama. Miss Battle told Ruby Dean to go on back to her seat, but when Ruby Dean did, Nettie started crying all over again.

"What is it now?" Miss Battle squawked, and the little girl said she would be quiet if she could sit next to Ruby Dean.

"Go ahead, then!" Miss Battle hollered, but this time Miss Battle sounded like she was going to cry.

Later that day, Miss Battle said to Ruby Dean in front of the class, "Ruby, I see you are good with children," and Ruby Dean looked all bashful. Then Miss Battle said in a real sweet voice (and we kids couldn't believe it was Miss Battle speaking), "Ruby, would you like to assist me with the first-graders at recess?" And Ruby Dean said, "Yes, ma'am," with a big ol' sunshine smile on her face. That day everybody went home happy.

When I told Mama about the little girl and Ruby Dean, Mama said Ruby Dean showed true Christian charity and she hoped Miss Battle had learned something from Ruby Dean's kindness.

I found something out about Miss Battle that makes me think she's not so bad after all. She keeps little packages of fruit and nuts and sweet bread in her desk drawer to give to the children who don't have any food to bring from home. She thinks nobody sees her slipping it to them at recess time when all the kids are running and playing and making noise. When lunchtime rolls around the children pull out their snacks like it came from home. I guess Miss Battle doesn't want them to feel bad about being poor.

When I told mama about it she said most everybody in Richmond County is poor, colored and white alike, except for people like the Cantwells and the Kestenbaums and the Delacroixes, who came up from New Orleans some years ago. And one or two well-to-do negroes. But she said some are poorer than others and its very kind of Miss Battle to look out for those children and for me to keep my mouth shut about it.

I still don't understand Miss Battle— after she does good she goes right back to being mean. I guess that's all the news

about school for now. Say hello to your
brother for me.

 From your best helper girl,

 Viney

September 20, 1929

Dear Viney,

 I hope this letter finds you and the family
doing well. I was sorry to hear about your new
teacher leaving so soon. Maybe she will return
to Richmond County someday. Miss Battle is a
fine teacher too. She is stern but that is because
she wants you children to learn so bad, not
because she is mean. I have known Irene Battle for
a long, long time. She comes from a fine family
of quality negroes who were house servants for
the Landy family. People who taught their slaves
how to read and write, something uncommon
and against the law in those days.

 Yes, Miss Battle was born in bondage same as I
was, and we were both still young children when
freedom came. And since most all the Landy
slaves knew how to read and write already when

they were freed, many of them were put to use by the Freedmen's Bureau as instructors, helping others learn to read and write.

So you see, Viney, Miss Battle knows how important education really is, and she's been teaching for a very long time. Please give her my regards. I hope you will still like school. Schooling is very important, so learn how to read well, Viney. The world is changing all the time.

Give a special hello to Charles for me. Tell him to write another letter and let me know how he is doing in school. Don't you two fight. And don't you forget to memorize your roots and herbs so you won't forget all I taught you this summer. Remember the game we used to play when we'd come in from the woods?

Give all the family my love. Tell your daddy to stay off that foot as much as he can. And again I thank him for looking after Duke and the cow. Hope to hear from you again soon. Be a good girl and say your prayers.

Yours very truly,
Missy Violet

MISS BATTLE AND THE SHARECROPPERS

Not long after Missy Violet wrote to me about Miss
Battle, some of the sharecropper farmers came to school
with Mister Waters and ganged up on Miss Battle. They
were upset because Miss Battle has been giving us a lot
of homework, a lot of reading and writing. She says we
must get ready for the essay contest. The sharecropper
farmers say so much homework keeps their children
from getting their chores done on the farm.

Mister Waters did most of the talking. He got real
loud again, just like he did with Miss Glover. But Miss
Battle, she can talk loud too. She dressed Mister Waters
down good fashioned in front of the class. Told him

that colored folks were doing fine things every day now. Becoming doctors and lawyers and teachers and inventors because they were able to get education.

"Let these children get their lessons out, man! And stop being a stumbling block!" she shouted at him. She said we might not all get educated, but some of us would, and I think her words must have scorched Mister Waters like hot coals because he stopped fussing and left. He even let Cleveland stay in class that day. Hooray for Miss Battle!

When Mister Waters left Miss Battle talked to us for a while about sharecroppers. She said she didn't want us to get the wrong idea about men like Mister Waters. She said he was a good man but he just couldn't believe that things were going to get better for colored people. She said he just didn't understand how important education was. "There are lots of people like that, children," Miss Battle told us. "But that doesn't mean that things won't change."

Miss Battle said that men like Mister Waters were smart men with their own brand of education. Instead of getting their knowledge from school and books they got their knowledge from life, which means that they know a lot of things. Miss Battle said that the sharecropper is a mechanic because he has to know how to fix farm machinery if he has any and if he doesn't he still has to know how to repair harnesses and shoes for his horses and mules.

She said he is part blacksmith, carpenter, animal trainer, and breeder. He has to know about all kinds of trees and the crops that grow on his land. He has to know something about insects and plant diseases and sprays to control insects. He even has to be a midwife and a doctor to the animals on the farm. And then she told us how a sharecropper farmer saved her neighbor's cow.

She said one day her neighbor's cow was eating some apples and she was gobbling them up so fast without chewing them and an apple got stuck in her throat. A sharecropper farmer was passing by in his wagon and saw the cow choking. The farmer took a piece of rubber hose, put a stick through it, and pushed it down the cow's throat but it didn't move the apple. So the farmer pushed his hand down the cow's throat and got hold of the apple and pulled it out. The cow didn't like it at all and stepped on the farmer's foot. But if the farmer had not done that the cow would have died.

"Sharecroppers and farmers are very special people, and I don't want you children to forget it," Miss Battle said. It sure was a surprise to hear Miss Battle put in a good word for Mister Waters and the sharecroppers. Miss Battle is beginning to sound a bit like Miss Glover . . .

Always Go Straight
Home from School

I don't know why, but I keep getting into trouble lately. Right after I got into hot water with Mama about writing that letter to Missy Violet about Miss Olette's daughter, I got into trouble again following behind Charles. This time I really did get a whupping—the worst I ever had. The trouble started one day while some of us kids were passing by the church on our way home from school. Charles said he knew a big secret about something that was inside the church. But before anybody could ask what it was, Charles blurted out, "It's a dead body!"

"Why don't you quit fibbin'," Arma Jean said, because she knows how Charles likes to make up stories. Nobody ever believes him except maybe Jeff Brown. He thinks Charles is the greatest thing since sliced bread.

"Why don't you tell the truth sometimes and shame the devil," I said to Charles, and his face started getting all red.

"If you don't believe me, why don't you go inside and see for yourself!" he told me.

"Y'all wanna go inside and see?" Cleveland asked, and silly us went inside. Arma Jean, Cleveland, Jeff Brown, Charles, and me. Ruby Dean was the smart one that day and went on home.

The church door was locked so we had to climb in through a window. "The Lord gonna punish us for this," Arma Jean said when our feet hit the floor.

"Aw, we ain't gonna touch nothin'—we jus' gonna look," said Charles.

"Yeah, yeah, we jus' gonna look," squawked Jeff Brown.

The lights inside the church were off, but we could still see the long, shiny black casket with the silver handles standing before the pulpit. We all stayed close together and walked up to the casket.

"Wow!" Cleveland whispered.

"Didn't I tell ya! Didn't I tell ya!" Charles hollered.

"Shhhhhh! We in church!" I reminded Charles.

"Dontcha wanna go up and see who it is?" he whispered, but his voice made an echo in the church.

"Noooo!" Arma Jean and I both said at the same time.

"I wanna see!" squawked Jeff Brown.

"Hush! You not suppose to disturb the dead," Arma Jean said.

"Yeah. They might come back and haunt you," Cleveland said.

"No they won't," said Charles, like he knew all about dead people.

"How you know?" asked Cleveland.

"'Cause the Good Book say, 'The dead know not anything.' So how is he gonna know who lookin' at him?" Charles answered.

"Where it say that?" Cleveland wanted to know.

"Missy Violet read it to me from the Bible so I wouldn't be afraid of the dead," Charles answered.

"We still got no business in here disturbin' this dead man," Arma Jean said.

"Y'all a buncha scaredy-cats!" Charles said, and laid his hand on top of the casket. Then he slid his hand back and forth, back and forth. "Man, this feel smooth and slick like a brand-new Cadillac," he said, showing off. Then Cleveland went over and touched the casket, then Jeff Brown, then Arma Jean, then me. I don't know why I touched it. I guess I did it because Arma Jean did.

"I bet you a quarter you won't lift up the lid," Cleveland dared Charles.

"It's a bet!"

"I hate boys," Arma Jean said. "Always darin' each other and showin' off."

Just then, Charles, Mister Biggity Showoff, lifted up the lid. It made a loud CLICK, and a smell like old flowers and turpentine floated up from the casket. And even with the lights off we got a good look at the dead man inside. He was very big and long, and his skin was the color of Brazil nut shells. He had on the nicest suit I'd ever seen on a colored man, and a ring with a large red stone was on his pinkie finger. Charles touched his face. "He feels cold and hard," he said. Then he laid his hand on the dead man's chest and frowned. "Feels like tissue paper," he said. Then all of us were touching the dead man's chest and face and hands. Arma Jean and I jerked our hands away when we touched his chest because it did feel all crinkly like tissue paper.

Charles said that he'd heard that sometimes the undertaker scoops out all of the dead person's insides and stuffs them with tissue paper so they wouldn't be so heavy. Ugh!

All at once, Mister Charles Elister Paxton Nehemiah Windbush Biggity Showoff reached in the casket and pulled the dead man's eyelids up. He must have accidentally twisted the dead man's head too, because all at once his head wasn't facing up toward the ceiling anymore but was facing us! Big, mean, scary gray eyes were staring right at us! Somebody slammed the casket lid down, and we scattered all over the church. Arma Jean and I finally got through the window. I got a splinter in my knee going over the sill.

It turned out the dead man was kin to a lady named Miss Willa Sumter, who lived on the outskirts of town, and he was a gangster who lived up north in Chicago. The undertaker's helper said he had been shot.

That Saturday at the funeral when the casket was opened for the family to have "the last look" there was the dead man, lying there facing the congregation. Starin' at them with those scary gray eyes just the way he had stared at us. They say Miss Willa fainted and some of the people ran out of the church.

Soon word got around, thanks to Miss Nula Irish, that the body had been "tampered with," especially since Miss Nula claimed she saw "a redheaded scamp and a gang of rascals" running from the church on Friday afternoon. The news got back to Mama, and Mama remembered that I'd gotten a splinter in my knee that I couldn't explain. She put two and two together and came after me with Papa's shavin' strap. Oh Lordy!

Charles Gets His Comeuppance

I know Charles is my first cousin and all, but I wish his ma would get well so he could go on back up to Mount Gilead. Papa says he doesn't think Aunt Charlotte will ever get well. He thinks there's something wrong with her heart. He says she's been sick ever since she was a little girl. He said if she ran and played too much she'd get tired and faint and their mama would have to hold smelling salts under her nose. Papa said most of the time she just sat on the porch in the rocker and tattled on the other children.

One time I dreamed Charles found some redheaded, freckle-faced people just like himself and moved far, far away. When I told Mama I wished that dream would come true, she said I got to be nice to Charles and show Christian charity because he's a guest in our home and he's our kin. Sometimes I wonder if Aunt Charlotte and Uncle Nehemiah just send him down here to get rid of him. I wouldn't blame them if they did. Mama says they sent him down here so he can be with his cousins because there are no children up there for him to be with. I think the children up there just don't like him.

Sometimes we'll be getting along just fine, but then he'll go and do something mean and spoil everything. Like the other day when nobody was looking, he cuffed me upside the head because he's still mad about what I said in the letter to Missy Violet about the cow patty. He's becoming a real bully. Mostly he picks on girls or boys like Jasper Kelly and Arthur Jones. Jasper's got a funny leg and Arthur's got a birthmark over one eye.

Charles is always making fun of them. "Where you get that ol' crooked leg from?" he says to Jasper, and Jasper's eyes fill up with water. Or he'll smack poor Arthur across the eye and say, "Oops, I thought that was a doodlebug settin' on your eye!" Sometimes he pushes them into each other to make the other kids laugh.

But somebody fixed Charles's business real good in school the other day, and it was Ruby Dean Baker! She had an apple on her desk and Charles kept foolin' with it—acting like he was going to snatch it off Ruby Dean's desk and eat it. Ruby Dean kept telling him to stop, but nobody hardly pays Ruby Dean any mind, she's so easygoing. But that day Ruby Dean meant it. So when Charles grabbed the apple and took a great big bite out of it, Ruby Dean clobbered him. She wrestled him to the floor, bopped him in the eye, and pounded him good. She was all over him like a net.

Miss Battle didn't say one word, just sat at her desk marking papers. And I shouldn't say this because Mama says it's a sin to laugh when your enemy gets his comeuppins, but I was glad, glad, glad! That big ol' Ruby Dean might not be so bright when it comes to learning, but she sure can wallop a bully! Now everybody wants to be her friend.

The only friend Charles has left is Jeff Brown, and Jeff's own mama says Jeff's head is not crowded with brains. But Jeff thinks Charles is the "bee's knees" because he's got freckles and red hair. He tells Charles, "I ain't never seen no colored boy like you before. You must be some kinda lucky!" And Charles just swells up. He's got Jeff thinking he can do anything.

Besides Jeff Brown and Missy Violet, the only other person who likes Charles is Cleo, my baby sister—and that's because she's only a few months old. But she sure cottons to Charles. Whenever he chucks her under the chin, she coos and grins. And her little baby eyes say, "I love you, Cousin Charles."

What We Saw in the Woods

Not long after Ruby Dean Baker whupped Charles good in class, he tried to make up with me.

"Hey, cuz, wanna play jacks?" he asked.

"Nope. Don't wanna play no jacks," I answered.

"Wanna play cards?"

"Nope."

"Well, how 'bout we go fishin', then."

Now, he had me when he said "go fishing." I loved fishing. Besides, I could fish circles around Charles. So that Saturday after we finished our chores we started out for our favorite fishing spot on the Pee Dee River. "Let's take the shortcut through the woods," Charles said. But

I didn't want to go through the woods with Charles, because every time I go through the woods with him he gets all crazy and tries to scare me. We'll be walking along and he'll just disappear. Or he'll make scary noises or jump out from somewhere shouting, "LOOK OUT! THE RAUSY BOYS!" or "HERE COMES HAIRY ESAU!" And I almost run over myself trying to get away. One time I fell down and busted my lip and skinned both knees, he scared me so bad.

"No," I said. "You gonna try and scare me."

"No I ain't," Charles promised. I don't know why I was stupid enough to believe him. I guess I really, really wanted to go fishing. Or maybe it was because I always hear Mama say, "Forgive those who trespass against us." But something happened in the woods that day that was a lot scarier than Charles.

The sun was nice and warm when we left, and the fish were jumping high. I caught seven catfish and two bass. Charles only caught four sunfish. My mouth was watering as I thought about those fish fryin' in Mama's big black skillet. But on the way back home, we walked up on something real, real scary: the Ku Klux Klan.

The Ku Klux Klan are a bunch of bad white men who

go around beating up colored people, or anybody who is not white. They even kill people. Mama and Papa said they were the ones who killed Uncle Bud, Papa's great-uncle, because he tried to vote for the Republican Party.

All the men had on white robes with hoods covering their heads, and they were standing around in a circle. At first we thought they were stringing somebody up, but then we saw that they were just talking and having some kind of meeting. Some children were with them, too — three boys. One of them looked like he was only five or six years old. Charles left me and jumped in the bushes, but I was too scared to move, and one of the men saw me. "Hey, gal, what you up to!" he hollered. I couldn't see his face, but I knew that voice. "I'm not doin' nothing, Mista Lordnorth," I answered. Mister Lordnorth's the man who owns the biggest furniture store in town.

"STUPID!" I heard Charles squawk in the bushes. "Now they gonna string us up for sure, 'cause you done pegged one of 'em." When Charles said that my knees began to knock and I could just see me and Charles swinging from a tall oak tree.

"Who in them bushes?" one of the men shouted as he went over and pulled Charles out of the mulberry bush.

I could tell that Charles was scared because his eyes were as big as wagon wheels. "Well, well, well, what have we here," said a great big Ku Klux man. I think he must have been the leader, because he wore a special hood and his robe had a big red circle with a white cross in the middle. He made us give him our fish and told us to "skedaddle." But the man with Mister Lordnorth's voice told him they couldn't let us go.

"Well, what we gonna do with 'em?" the man asked. And the man with Mister Lordnorth's voice said something to the leader man, and they tied us up and went back to what they were doing. Charles and I started to cry. "Viney, they gonna kill us!" Charles kept saying, and every time he said it my stomach hurt. I started wondering what it would feel like when they killed us and what it would feel like to be dead and never to see Mama and Papa again. I was crying so hard, my nose started to run, but I couldn't wipe it because my hands were tied and that made me cry even more.

I could hear Charles praying and I tried to pray, too, but the words kept getting all mixed up. I wondered if God could hear us way down there in the woods. I closed my eyes real tight, trying to pray, but all I could see was Charles and me laid out in two white caskets, like the one they had for Miss Daisy Mack's little girl when she died of the diphtheria. Two small-size white caskets standing in front of the pulpit at the church, and Mama and Papa and Aunt Charlotte and Uncle Nehemiah just crying their hearts out.

I wanted Papa to come and get me. I wanted him to ride up on his horse and snatch me and Charles up on his saddle and ride away. "Oh, Papa, Papa, Papa!" I kept crying, and when I opened my eyes one of the little boys who was with the Ku Klux was standing there looking at us. He had big blue eyes that looked like two blue marbles, and he just stared and stared at us. Then he did a curious thing—he untied our hands.

"Hey," he said when we were untied.

"Hey," we said back.

"My name is Jody and y'all better run," he said. And we did. We ran as fast as we could. It was just like a miracle in the Bible how that little boy helped us get away. But I wondered what made him do it. I wondered how his little fingers untied that heavy rope. Jody . . . Jody . . .

Jody. I kept saying his name in my head all the way home so I wouldn't forget it. And I kept hoping that those bad men would never find out what he did.

When we got home we told Mama and Papa what had happened to us, and Mama started crying and thanking the Lord for saving us from the Klan. When we told them the part about Mister Lordnorth, Mama had to sit down. "Those the same men who give us a ride home after we done worked in their wives' kitchens and fed their children," she said. "The same men be underneath those white sheets! The same men who wait on us in the stores be hidin' under those hoods, 'cause they don't want folks to know who they are. Some of their own family members don't even know they belong to the Klan!"

Mama said we'd never set foot in Mister Lordnorth's store again even though he was good about letting colored people have credit. But the last thing she said on the matter was "Lord, bless that little white boy's sweet baby heart."

For a long time after that happened I had bad dreams about Mister Lordnorth and I was afraid to go into town with Mama and Papa on Saturdays. I was afraid Mister

Lordnorth would see me and send the Klan to get me out of my bed one night or burn a cross in front of our house.

Papa said not to worry so much about it, that all colored children looked the same to Mister Lordnorth. He said if he was going to remember anyone it would be Charles because of his red hair. That made me feel a little better, but not much. I didn't want them to get Charles either. I hope God will save us from the Ku Klux again the way He did when we were tied up down in the woods.

TELLING ALL ABOUT OUR TROUBLES

September 22, 1929
Dear Missy Violet,

I just had to write you again and tell you about the terrible thing that happened to Charles and me when we went fishing this past Saturday. We took a shortcut to the Pee Dee river. But we walked up on the Ku Klux having a secret meeting. They saw us and made us turn over our fish. They tied us up because I recognized Mister Lordnorth when he spoke even though his face was covered up with a hood. We were so scared. I thought they would kill us for sure. I thought I would never see you or Mama and Papa again. Charles left me and jumped in the bushes, though he's been telling folks that he fought the Klan off.

But the truth is, he cried and prayed so hard and pitiful, I couldn't even get mad at him. I was crying and praying, too. Then, Missy Violet, a good thing happened. There were some boys in the woods with those men. One was only about five or six years old. A little boy with blue eyes. He came over and untied us. His name was Jody. He said, "Y'all better run." I pray for little Jody every night, because he saved us.

My brothers want to go get Mister Lordnorth, but they know better. Mama wants them to keep quiet about what happened. She doesn't want any trouble. She and Papa finally got the boys to calm down, all except Claude Thomas. You know how Claude Thomas is, Missy Violet. He says he is going to kill one of the Klan.

Mama is so afraid for him, she is thinking
about sending him away. Mama told him
about little Jody saving us, but it didn't
do any good. He's mad at all white people.
I wish I could understand why all different
kinds of people can't love each other.

Charles try to pretend he's not scared.
He says he is going to tell Mister
Lordnorth that his great-granddaddy on his
mama's side was white and he thinks that
that will keep the Klan from bothering him.
Papa told him if he knows what's good for
him he'd better keep his mouth shut! Please
pray for us and please write soon.

Viney

September 22, 1929
Deer Missy Violet,

Its me again writin to tell you what happen
to me and Viney in the woods comin from the
P.D. riva. Me and Viney went fishin and I
catched a lot of fish, twiney or thurdy.
Viney just catched a few sunfish. She think

She such a good fisher but I can catch more thin her any time. Any how we come back thru the woods. It was Viney's idea. And guess what, Missy Violet? We walk right up on the Klan. They was wearin white sheets and hoods and evything, and befo we could hide they seen us.

One of the men under the hoods was Mr. Lordnorf who own the firniture store. Viney went and called out his name, thin he new she new who he was and they tied us up. Viney was just hollerin and cryin and callin on the Lord. I tole her to hush but she woodint shut-up. You know she is a real scurdy cat.

You wooda ben proud of me. I was brave and strong. I thought and thought and thought of a way to save us. Then I did like Tom Mix did when those outlaws tied him up in that cowboy movie. He rubbed the rope aginst the tree and cut his sef loose. Then I untied Viney and we ran home. Viney so scired Mr. Lordnorf gonna come and git her. Unca James tole her not to worry, he said all colard chiren look the same to Mr. Lordnorf excep maybe me. He said he wood remember my red hair. Do you think he will? If he do he might come and git me out my bed one nite and carry me in the woods and string me up! And mama and papa won't neva see me again.

Missy Violet, I hope you can come home soon, becose you know most all the white folks in the county and you done helped bring some of their chiren in the worl. So maybe you could talk to Mr. Lordnorf and tell him I am not a bad kid and if he want me to I will work in his store for free.

Please write back qwik!

Charles

WORDS TO COMFORT

September 27, 1929

Dear Viney, Dear Charles,

My dumplings, Missy Violet was so sorry to hear about the terrible thing that happened to you in the woods. It is sad that people do bad things to one another, but that's the way the world has been ever since Adam turned his back on God.

Thank the Good Lord for that little boy, Jody. I think I know who he is. I believe he belongs to Mr. Lordnorth's daughter, Laura Lee. She is married to one of the Delacroixes. I did not attend his birth but I remember when that little boy was born. He is the Lordnorths' only grandchild. I know the family quite well — I used to make tonics and teas for Mrs. Lordnorth. And there was a time when Mr. Lordnorth wanted to go into business with me. He wanted to sell my teas and tonics, but to do that would have taken up too much of my time and I wanted to care for my patients.

Try to get over what happened, children. Try not to let hate grow in your hearts — look what it has done to Claude Thomas, your brother. Hate has eaten him up. There is a better time coming. Look to that time. Be peaceable, do good works — it is like a salve that heals. Be kind to all. This will keep you steady.

I don't think you children need to worry about Mr. Lordnorth. Just stay out of his way. I think his main concern is making a lot of money. Your main concern should be getting an education. Be good students. Make Miss Battle proud. Stay out of the woods for a while if you can.

I hope to be home before the year is out and

am looking forward to seeing you two. Give the family my regards, and you two try to get along in Christian love.

Yours very truly,

Missy Violet

SAVANNAH

My big sister, Savannah, just saw her eighteenth birthday and wants to start keeping company. Most girls around here start courting at fifteen, but Papa said Savannah couldn't start seeing boys until she got some education. Some folks say Papa is uppity for thinking that way. They say, "Who does James Windbush think he is? Savannah just gonna marry and have a house full a children like her mama." And Papa says, "Yeah, but she'll be able to teach 'em to read and write."

Two boys have already come by the house trying to get Papa's permission to walk Savannah home from church on Sundays, Lorendo Smith and Solomon

Trueheart. Savannah's sweet on Solomon but Papa favors Lorendo because Lorendo's father is partners with Mister Brownlee, the colored undertaker. They've been grooming Lorendo for the undertaking business and Papa thinks that's a fine thing. "I don't want my girls marryin' no sharecroppers," Papa is always saying. Solomon's father is a sharecropper.

Lorendo is all right. He is tall and noble-looking, but Solomon's got maroon-colored eyes and black wavy hair that shines like a crow's feathers. Papa says, "All them pretty-boy good looks are not what matters." He says what matters is what's inside a man and how he looks at the world. Mama disagrees with Papa and they go back and forth with this all the time, like two pups tussling over a bone. Mama says good looks *do* matter, if you don't want your grandchildren to be hard on the eyes.

Papa thinks Lorendo is a smart fella and has a good handle on things. He likes the way Lorendo works at the funeral home on the weekends and in the summer when school is out. Papa also says Lorendo doesn't smoke cigarettes or get into mischief like other boys do, although we never heard of Solomon getting into mischief either.

The day Solomon stopped by, Papa was sitting on the

porch with his injured foot up on a footstool. Solomon looked very nice even though it was only a weekday. His shirt was pressed, his shoes were shined, and he had on new overalls. He came up on the porch and removed his hat. "How do, Mista Windbush, sir? How is the missus?" He tried to make his voice sound all deep and important.

"Somethin' wrong with ya throat, boy?" Papa growled.

"Oh, no, sir," Solomon answered. "Just askin' how you and the missus?" Papa's face balled up in a knot—he didn't even invite Solomon to sit down.

"I be just fine," Papa finally grunted. "The missus, she fine too." Solomon cleared his throat and held on tight to his hat.

"Mista Windbush, sir," Solomon said, "I'm here to ask permission to walk Savannah home from church service on Sundays." Papa would have swallowed his chewing tobacco if he had known Solomon was already walking Savannah home from school every day.

Papa give Solomon the fish eyes and wouldn't answer him a word. Poor Solomon just stood there squirming.

"What you say, boy?" Papa barked, and Solomon repeated what he'd said, but this time his voice came out all high and squeaky. Savannah and I were standing on the other side of the screen door, watching. We clapped our hands over our mouths to keep from laughing, because Solomon had the same look on his face that Daisy, our mule, gets when she's been spooked.

All of a sudden Solomon started speaking in his regular voice that he used at school every day. "I'd like your permission to walk Savannah home from church on Sundays, sir?" he asked.

"Why you wanna walk my daughter home from church?" Papa asked, and I felt sorry for Solomon. Papa was being so mean to him.

"Just wantin' to be social, sir. That's all," Solomon answered.

"Solomon likes to discuss Reverend Mim's sermons after service, Papa," Savannah put in from the other side of the screen door. And her voice reminded me of a bird warbling.

"What's your intentions?" Papa asked in that gruff, mean voice again.

"I'd like to get to know Savannah and her family better, Mista Windbush," Solomon said, and I thought that was a nice thing for him to say.

"For what?" Papa barked.

And Solomon said real nice and polite, "Well, sir, to be her friend and to talk and listen to her."

"Oh yeah?" Papa said in a way that sounded like he didn't believe Solomon.

Then Solomon began to pour out his heart to Papa. "Mista Windbush, sir, you done raised a fine girl, and if things go right maybe someday Savannah will be my wife."

"Wife!" I thought Mama would have to come and put Papa's eyeballs back in his head.

"Yes, sir, I hopes to take a wife someday. And I hope to be the kind of person she can come to, and to be someone who can comfort her in hard times."

Papa's mouth dropped open like a trapdoor. I don't think he expected Solomon to be so bold.

"Humph," Papa grunted.

"And I'd like you to know, sir, that I'll be graduating from school this spring and I plan to go on to normal school and then on to agricultural college when I graduate." This made Papa sit back in his chair, and some of the worry lines on his face smoothed out. "That so?" Papa said, and his voice sounded almost nice. I thought Savannah would burst open, she was so proud.

"Will you give your permission, sir?" Solomon asked. And Papa started pulling on his chin, the way he does when he's thinking about something real hard.

"Well, I don't know," Papa said.

"I'm a respectable fella, Mista Windbush," Solomon said. "I don't drink no hard liquor. I don't shoot craps, and I don't smoke."

"Well, I know that's true about the smokin'," Papa mumbled, "'cause I never seen you up there at Liggett and Meyers, tryin' to bum free cigarettes."

"Please, Papa!" Savannah squealed.

"You ain't gonna sully my girl's good name, is you?" Papa asked Solomon, and gave him a hard look.

"Why, no, sir! Noooo, nooo," Solomon answered.

"You best not to," Papa said. "'Cause if you do, I'll get my gun and I'll—"

"James!" It was Mama. We hadn't even heard her walk up, but there she was, standing in the doorway. "Why you tantalizin' the life outta this boy? You gonna let him walk Savannah home from church or not?" Papa gave Mama a look and I knew there would be some words said later on at the supper table.

So Papa gave his permission, but only for third

Sundays. So now on every third Sunday, Solomon Trueheart walks my sister Savannah home from church.

That night while Savannah and I were in bed I asked her about boys. She laughed and said, "What you want to know, kitten? Are you in love?"

"Ugh, no! I hate boys," I said. "I just want to know how it feels when you are in love." And Savannah laughed, a pretty, tinkly, silvery laugh. "It feels real nice," she said. "You feel all warm and safe inside. And when you say his name it taste like honey on your tongue."

"Ugh, that's enough!" I put my hands over my ears. "You and Solomon gonna get married?" I asked.

"I sure hope so," Savannah said.

LORENDO

Lorendo came by our house last week. He rode up on a fine reddish-brown horse they call a bay stallion. The horse's name is Socrates. Lorendo says he named him that because he's real smart. If he were my horse I would name him Socks because his ankles are as white as snow and it looks like he's wearing socks. Sometimes, Lorendo lets us kids scratch between Socrates's ears and rub his nose.

Papa rushed out on the porch when he saw Lorendo coming. "Lorendo! How you, boy!" Papa shouted, and hollered for Savannah to come out and sit on the porch. I never saw Papa so excited. When Savannah came out,

Mama was with her, so Lorendo tipped his hat. "How do, ma'am," he said to Mama, then he bowed to Savannah. He did it just the way those cowboys do in the Tom Mix movies, when they ride up on a horse and meet a lady.

Savannah gave him a crooked little smile. "Hey, Lorendo," she said. But it wasn't like the greeting she gives Solomon. She gives Solomon a great big ol' Mary Sunshine smile.

"Come on up on the porch and set a spell," Papa told Lorendo, and he came up on the porch and sat down and stretched his long legs. He was wearing a fine pair of leather boots. When I stuck my head out the door to say hello, Papa hissed, "Scat!" before I could say a word. I had to duck right back inside. I suspect Papa was scared I might say something about Solomon in front of Lorendo. But Charles was the one he should have been worried about—he's the one who let the cat out of the bag that Reverend Mims wears a toupee.

Right away Papa started asking Lorendo about the funeral business and Lorendo commenced to bragging about all his duties at the funeral home.

"Excuse me, Lorendo," Savannah interrupted him in a voice sweet as molasses, "but Mama and I got a heap of ironin' waitin' on us inside. Please excuse us. Excuse me, Papa," Savannah said, and did a little curtsy to Papa, but Papa just waved his hand at her.

"That ironin' not goin' nowhere, girl. Set down," he said.

Savannah looked to Mama for help, and Mama said, "That's the point, James. The ironin' not goin' anywhere unless we get to it. You want wrinkled shirts all week?" Then Mama nodded good day to Lorendo and she and Savannah went back inside.

I heard Savannah say about Lorendo when she got back inside the house, "That rooster think the sun comes up just to hear him crow."

Papa was hissin' like a teakettle, he was so mad! But he didn't say a word to Mama, even later after he came back into the house, because he and Lorendo had a slick little trick up their sleeves to break Savannah and Solomon up.

GETTING READY FOR THE CONTEST

October 7, 1929
Dear Missy Violet,
  Thank you for the nice letter. It made
Charles and me feel better. We have not
been back in the woods, but we passed
by Mister Lordnorth's store one Saturday.
We were in Papa's wagon. We ducked
down when Papa drove by the store. I have
not had any bad dreams about the woods
anymore. Mama said we should stop talking
about it, but Charles is still bragging about

what a hero he was in the woods. Nobody believes him except Jeff Brown.

Anyway, I'm writing to tell you about the essay contest—it's almost time. Everybody is excited and a little scared because Miss Battle is making us read our essays in front of the class. Arma Jean, Cleveland, Charles, and I have been working on our essays all week. Charles keeps trying to see what I wrote about, but he won't let me near his paper.

Arma Jean is writing about her mama's new washing machine. Cleveland is writing about some trees he read about in the Bible. Charles says he's going to write about his trip to New York City, and me, I'm writing about my summer helping you "catch babies." All of us except Charles are sending you a copy.

This is Arma Jean's essay:

This summer my mama got a new washer machine. It's not really new. It belonged to

Miss Letty the white lady my mama work for. Miss Letty got a brand-new washer machine and she give the old one to mama. It looks like a big pickle barrel. Mama sure was glad to get it because mama got nine children to wash for. Daddy picked it up in his wagon and put it on the back porch. It goes chooka, chooka, chooka, chooka, chooka, chooka, chook.

The clothes smell so good washing in it.

Now Mama don't have to boil the clothes in those big iron pots no more and use that lye soap that ruins her hands. Now we use soap powders.

Mama lets us children take turns running the clothes through the wringer that squeezes the water out. Now everybody want to help Mama wash. It must have been some smart man who made the washer machine. The way he got the tub to wobble back and forth and the thing called the agitator to spank those clothes clean.

Mama's clothes look so pretty and clean hanging on the line. They looked pretty and clean when she boiled them too, but now all my sisters are fighting over who is going to help Mama wash every week. Before, Mama couldn't find anybody to help when it was wash day. She had to go after them with the switch.

I like Arma Jean's essay. It makes me want to see how a washing machine works. I wonder who made the first washing machine? I wish my mama would get one.
Here is Cleveland's essay:

My name is Cleveland Waters and since I didn't do nothing this summer but plow and feed the hogs and chickens, my essay is going to be about trees. I like trees, all kinds of trees. I like to look at the different kinds of leaves that grow on trees. But the trees I am going to write about are not the trees that grow here in Richmond County but some trees I read about in the Holy Bible.

In the Bible trees sometimes stand for people and kings and nations. There are many different kinds of trees in the Bible. Like the Tree of Knowledge of Good and Bad and the Tree of Life. Jesus talked about trees in his parables. He talked about the fig tree and the tree that puts forth good fruit. He talked about trees that were no good and should be cut down. But the trees that I am going to write about are trees that talked and acted like people.

In the Book of Judges there was a bramble tree, an olive tree, a fig tree, and a vine. One day the trees asked the olive tree to be king over them. But the olive tree said it didn't want to give up its fatness to be king over the other trees, so they asked the fig tree to be queen over them. And the fig tree said she didn't want

to leave her sweetness to be queen over
them. So they asked the vine and the vine
said no too, because it didn't want to leave
its wine to rule over them.

So then all the trees got together and
asked the bramble to be king over them
and the bramble said yes. "Put your trust
in my shadow." But the funny thing about
that was the bramble tree was a short
tree that people only used for kindlin'
wood. I think this story was talking about
the kings and people back in early times,
but I don't know which ones.

I think I would like to be a preacher
when I grow up. Not the kind that holler
and stomp but the kind that teach people
the Bible.

Wasn't that a good story about trees?
My favorite story in the Bible is Daniel
in the lion's den. If I was Miss Battle I
would give Cleveland first prize.

Here is my essay:

This summer I learned where babies come from. I used to think they came out of tree stumps and cabbage patches. But your mama just tells you that so you won't get grown too fast. Babies come from inside their mothers. I can't explain how they get there, but I think it has something to do with the daddy. Then the midwife catches the baby when it comes out.

Miss Viola McCrae is the midwife in our community. Sometimes people call her the granny, but she doesn't mind. Most folks call her Missy Violet. She is like a doctor and knows how to make people feel better. She knows how to turn plants into medicine. I asked her how she learned so much and she said from her mother. She said her mother was the granny on a plantation back in slavery time and her mother used to take her in the woods with her to gather roots and herbs. So Missy Violet was a little girl when she started learning about plants.

Missy Violet showed me how to dry plants and grind them into tea. She has lots of plants in her kitchen hanging from the rafters and in a big glass cabinet. I liked learning about the plants and what they can be turned into like teas and creams and syrups, even candies. Missy Violet said the Lord made all these plants to help us.

Everybody keeps coming up to me asking me did I really see the babies come out of the mothers? And I have to say not exactly, but I was there. All I know is when we came to the house there was no baby and when we left there was a baby. Kicking and squalling all over the place. Sometimes I would sit on the bed and press the pillows behind the mama's back. If Missy Violet didn't need me I'd go outside and play with the other children. At other times Missy

Violet tells me to make tea or to slice up the sweet bread she makes. She always brings sweet bread for the family to eat and a little wine or brandy for the new papas to drink.

When Missy Violet and I are not catching a baby we visit the sick and shut-in. She takes them teas and poultices and creams. Sometimes she just sits and talks to them. I like that part of helping the sick. I like helping people get better. It gives me a good feeling inside. And I like to hold the new babies after they are born.

When Missy Violet cannot go herself she sends me to deliver medicine to the sick. I feel happy she can trust me to do a good job. One time when Missy Violet was away I helped another midwife catch a baby. Missy Violet was real proud of me.

I want to be a midwife or a nurse when I get big. I used to want to be a teacher. Both are important, both help people.

Missy Violet, what do you think? Did you like the essays? I hope all of us will get a good mark.

Yours truly,

Viney

Always Happy to Hear from You

October 15, 1929

Dear Viney,

I am always happy to hear from you children. I was really surprised when I received such a fat envelope. But I enjoyed reading every word of those fine essays you and Arma Jean and Cleveland sent. I read them to my brother and he enjoyed them very much. He was having a bad day but when I read him the essays I think they lifted his spirits. I know Miss Battle is going to be pleased. I am sure you will all get a high mark.

Where is Charles's essay? Tell him that I am waiting to hear from him. And encourage him to work on his spelling.

How is the family? How is your daddy's foot coming along? Are you still treating it with the cayenne liniment? I don't know if I mentioned it before, but I am so proud of the way you took charge when he had his accident. Keep up the good work. Give your sisters and your brothers my love and tell Arma Jean and Cleveland that when I come home we will all get together at my house one Saturday for some coconut cake and lemonade.

Please write and tell me who won the essay contest. God bless you sweet children.

Yours very truly,

Missy Violet

The Essay Contest

October 22, 1929

Dear Missy Violet,

Miss Battle held the essay contest this past week. It was on a Wednesday, part in the morning, part in the afternoon. Arma Jean and I thought she should have held it on a Friday so the losers wouldn't have to look at the winners the next day. Especially if somebody like Margie Poole or my cousin Charles won.

Miss Battle split the class up into three groups: lower, middle, and upper. Everybody had to read their essay in front of the class. The lowers read first. Those are the little ones who are just learning how to read and write. Most of them wrote one or two sentences about a pet or a toy, or the sun or the flowers. They were real cute. One little girl wet on herself when she got up to read.

Next was my group's turn. I was so nervous, I couldn't eat and I thought my stomach would fall out. I even asked Mama if I could stay home from school. Mama said, "Eat your breakfast, honey, you'll be all right. Besides, you have a new dress to wear."

"And new ribbons, too," Savannah said. I had forgotten about the new dress Savannah and Mama made for me to wear to the contest. At least I would look nice when I got up in front of the class.

"That's right, I get to wear my new dress today!" I said, and tried to sound all excited because I didn't want to hurt

Savannah's or Mama's feelings. Mama and Savannah smiled.

When I got to school Arma Jean met me in the schoolyard.

"You scared?" she asked.

"Yeah. You?"

"A little," Arma Jean said. "You look nice."

"You do too. I like your hair," I told Arma Jean. She also had new ribbons.

Class started and Miss Battle asked who wanted to go first. Nobody raised a hand. So Miss Battle called on Winsome Blue. Winsome is the prettiest girl in my group. She is a good reader too, but this morning her eyes were all red like she'd been crying and her hands were shaking and her voice came out all squeaky. She looked like I felt. She read through her essay real fast, then rushed back to her seat and started to cry. Maybe she didn't read so well because Miss Battle called on her first.

Next Miss Battle called on Charles's

friend Jeff Brown. When Jeff got up to read, Charles started smacking himself on the head and making the other children laugh, but Jeff did better than we thought he would. Jeff's essay was about a trip down to New Orleans with his grandfather. When he sat back down Miss Battle said, "Very good, Jeff Brown. You surprised me."

She called Arma Jean up next. Arma Jean read her essay about her mama's new washing machine and she wasn't nervous at all. She was bold as sunshine, just like she always is. When Arma Jean sat back down, Miss Battle didn't say a word. I don't think Miss Battle likes Arma Jean very much. One time in front of the whole class she told Arma Jean she was "too forward." I guess that's because Arma Jean has a quick tongue and a smarty answer for everything. Some folks say she's got grown folks' sense. But she's still my best friend.

Cleveland was called up next and he read

his essay about the trees in the Bible.
I thought it was beautiful. Miss Battle
was smiling when Cleveland sat back down.
Margie Poole came up next. She walked up
to the front of the class all superior, like
she thought she was a queen. And Arma
Jean looked over at me and rolled her eyes.

Margie is one of the smartest kids in the
class, always raising her hand. She gets the
right answers too. Showoff! She even won
first prize last year in the essay contest.
But that's no reason for her to be all
stuck-up.

Margie read her essay like she was in
a play, throwing her hands all out to the
sides like she was on a stage, singing a
song. She even curtsied before she sat back
down. Her essay was about her visit to
the Statue of Liberty in New York City.
Arma Jean says she tells everybody she goes
up there to visit her grandparents, but
she really goes up there to see her father
because Mister Poole is not her real daddy.

"Thank you, Margie. That was well done," Miss Battle said when Margie sat back down. I bet she'll win first prize again this year.

Miss Battle called Charles up next. He always acts like a clown in class and tries to make people laugh. So he walked up to the front of the class with his hands folded like in prayer, then made like he forgot his essay and hurried back to his seat. Everybody laughed except Miss Battle.

Charles kept cutting up, but I could tell he was scared because of the way his eyes looked. His essay was about his trip to New York but he read it so fast, it didn't make much sense. He didn't look up from the paper one time, and he kept shuffling his feet. At the end he let out a great big sigh and hurried back to his seat. Miss Battle just rolled her eyes. She called me up next.

My stomach hurt, my knees wobbled, my hands got sweaty. And Margie Poole was looking at me with that smirk on her face. The look she had when I told her babies came out of a tree stump. My heart started pounding in my ears as I walked up to the front of the class. When I got up there I looked in the back to see if I could see my sister and my brothers. I did, and Savannah gave me a smile. Lincoln winked and Antonio made a silly face. All of that made me feel better. Claude Thomas just sat there looking out the window, but that was all right. He was still my brother.

Then all of a sudden, I couldn't see them anymore. Something was happening to my eyes—they felt like they were getting smaller and smaller. I could hear myself reading and my voice sounded a little funny, but at least I wasn't reading too fast. I stopped and started over again and my heart started to slow down.

I hoped I wasn't looking funny like Charles did when he was up there. I didn't want them to laugh at me. I felt hot circles growing around my eyes, but I was getting near to the end and I wasn't stuttering, so I was glad. Finished! Phew!

I went back to my seat and sat down. Miss Battle nodded her head. "Very nice, Viney," she said. I couldn't believe my ears. Miss Battle said my essay was "very nice." Maybe I wouldn't win a prize, but I could get a good mark. I took a deep breath. I felt good all over.

Cleveland won first prize for his essay about the Bible trees and the nice pictures he drew to go with it. He won a fountain pen and a bottle of India ink. *I won second prize!* A package of green writing paper with matching green envelopes, just what I need to write lots of letters to you, Missy Violet. Ruby Dean Baker won third prize, a set of composition books. She won for best effort and best penmanship. Her essay was sad—it was about her mama and papa getting drowned in a rowboat while they were out fishing and how she and her sisters and brothers had to come live with their grandma.

Ruby Dean didn't really read her essay—she mostly just told it. The class was real quiet while she was talking, even Charles. We all felt sorry about what had happened to her mama and papa. Maybe that's why Miss Battle gave her third prize. Margie Poole was soooo jealous. Arma Jean and Jeff Brown received As. I got an A. Charles got a C, mostly because of his bad spelling and his clowning.

Essay time is all over. Miss Battle said next month we will be doing a lot of arithmetic. I used to hate arithmetic, but now I want to learn it because I want to be a nurse or a midwife like you, Missy Violet. And I must be able to weigh and measure when I make tonics and poultices and catch babies. I have to know how to put in so much of this and so much of that. I am going to try to like arithmetic now.

Oh, Missy Violet, I almost forgot to tell you about the new girl. A new girl started school with us in August. Her name is Easter Brownlee and she is eleven years old. She said her mama named her Easter because she was born on an Easter Sunday. Mister Brownlee the undertaker is her uncle and she came to live with him and Missus Brownlee after her mama ran off with a married man. Everybody gathered around her at recess time because they all wanted to know what it is like to live in a funeral home.

Easter told us her uncle learned the undertaker business from his father, who learned it from his father, who was born in slavery time. His master used to hire him out to a white undertaker who lived in his town. She said the white undertaker used his stable for his undertaker business and he taught the slave "the business of the dead." That was just the way she said it: "the business of the dead."

She said she hated living in a funeral home. She said it gave her the creeps. She gave us the creeps too. "There's two bodies down in the basement right now while we standin' here talkin'," Easter told us.

"You ever see any of them dead folks down in the basement?" Charles asked, with his mouth hanging open like a catfish.

"My uncle took me down there to see a little girl one time," Easter said. "She just looked like she was sleepin'."

"Were you scared?" somebody asked.

"Yeah," the new girl said. Then Miss Battle came over and broke us up before she could tell us what happened.

"You wanna walk home together?" Charles asked the new girl as we were going back into the schoolhouse. He wanted to hear more about the dead people. Easter nodded her head yes. So Charles and I and Arma Jean and Cleveland and Jeff and Ruby Dean walked home from school with her.

Charles was full of questions as we walked along. "You ever hear them dead folks walkin' around down there in the basement?" he asked. "Do they really moan and groan while the undertaker workin' on 'em?"

But Easter cut him off with a question of her own. "Are you the kids who broke into the church and tampered with that body a few weeks ago?" she asked. Charles's face turned bright red. Arma Jean poked me with her elbow.

"What you got to say, Charles," Arma Jean said, all calm and cool.

"Oh, shut up, Arma Jean! Just shut up!" Charles squawked.

"Yeah, it was us," Arma Jean said. "But Charles was the ringleader."

"It wasn't a very smart thing to do. You

know you could go to jail for that. Or catch some kind of germ," the new girl said. And I knew I was going to like her from that day on, because she had made Charles look stupid—him and his prank. Miss Battle would call this girl "apt." I invited Easter to come to knitting lessons with Arma Jean and me when you get back from Florida, Missy Violet. I hope you don't mind. I think you will like Easter. She made Arma Jean and I see how lucky we are to be living in a regular house with regular people instead of in a funeral home with dead folks.

Please write back soon.

Your best helper girl,

Viney

October 30, 1929

Dear Viney,

A salute to you and your friends. You all worked hard on your essays, and see how it turned out? I am sure all of your parents are so proud. I hope you children will work just as hard for the rest of the year.

Where is Charles? Give him my love. Tell him to write me.

If all goes well, I should be home before the new year.

Yours very truly,

Missy Violet

A Sad Tale

We had some goings-on at our house early this morning!
Mama and Savannah were in the yard washing clothes
when Mary Lee Washington come stumbling by on her
way home from "an all-night drunk," Mama said. She
must have thought she was already home because she
stumbled up on our front porch and sat down on the
steps.

Mama went around to the steps and hollered at her
to get off our porch and go on home. "You ought to be
shame a yourself, Mary Lee. Drunk first thing in the
mornin'. An' you a new mother. You ought to be home

nursin' your baby!" Mama told her. When Mama said that, Mary Lee began to cry. I never saw anybody cry like that before, even when somebody died. It was like something broke loose deep down inside her and she was crying for the whole wide world.

Mama went and sat down beside her on the steps. "Mary Lee, I'm sorry. You know you shouldn't be out here like this and you just had a newborn baby," Mama said, and I could tell by the way Mama said it, she was real sorry. Mama put her arm around Mary Lee's shoulder. She asked Mary Lee who was at home with her baby and Mary Lee said the baby was with her mama and papa. "But why you not home with her?" Mama kept wanting to know.

"Miss Lena, you seen my baby?" Mary Lee asked.

"Girl, you know I never saw your baby," Mama answered. But Mama had heard about the baby, because people were whispering about it, saying it was malformed. Some said it had two heads and four arms. Some said it didn't have any arms at all. Mary Lee had named her Anna Rose.

"Miss Lena, my poor baby is malformed. She shaped

like a fish where she ought to have legs. But she got the sweetest face you ever did see," Mary Lee said. Then she began to cry again.

"Why, Miss Lena? Why? Why this happen to my baby?" Mary Lee asked.

Mama was quiet for a minute, then said, "These things just happen sometimes, Mary Lee. I'm so sorry it had to happen to you."

Mary Lee looked up at Mama. "I know why it happened, Miss Lena. I ain't been wantin' to say it out loud, but I know why this happened to me. The Lord, He punishin' me."

"No, Mary Lee, don't say that." Mama tried to hush her up.

"It's true," said Mary Lee. "The Lord punishin' me for all them bad things I done. You know, Miss Lena, I started drinkin' liquor and smokin' cigarettes when I was just twelve years old. Started foolin' 'round with boys and men when I was thirteen. Sassed my mama and papa when they tried to chastise me. Now all this done come back on my little baby."

I heard Mama suck in her breath. "What you think the Lord is, Mary Lee? A great big ol' bully, go 'round pickin' on little babies? No, honey—things just go wrong sometimes. The Good Book say, 'Chance happeneth to them all.' Everybody have bad things happen to them sometimes."

Later, when Mama came in the house, I told her I knew about some medicine that would make Mary Lee feel better. "How you know 'bout Mary Lee?" Mama asked, and I had to tell her that I was standing inside the screen door while they were talking and heard what they said.

"My baby, always just happen to be standin' somewhere listenin' in on grown folks' conversations?" Mama laughed.

"Now, what's this medicine you talkin' about?" Mama asked.

"I learned about it this summer when I was helping Missy Violet catch babies. It's called goldenseal, and I know what it looks like in the woods and everything, and I could get some for her and make her some tea. Missy Violet says it's good to calm the nerves, and she gives it to her skittish patients."

So the next day me and Mama went into the woods looking for goldenseal. It made me think about the times

I went into the woods with Missy Violet, and I was proud I was able to show Mama what I had learned. I was so glad I had paid attention when Missy Violet was teaching me about the roots and herbs. She always made a little game out of it by teaching me the nicknames of the different plants. It's easier to remember the nicknames, like skullcap or coltsfoot or skunk cabbage or shepherd's purse or devil's bones.

Mama and I kept walking in the woods. "There it is, Mama!" I hollered when I saw the plant. "See, the leaves have five sides. Three big sides and two little sides." I spread the leaves out so Mama could see. "Now, we take only what we need and leave a bunch so it will grow back next year," I said, trying to sound like Missy Violet, and grabbed two stems and yanked them out of the ground. I was so proud I could show Mama how to "gather."

"Look!" I hollered when the fat yellow root popped out of the ground.

"It looks almost like a carrot," Mama said.

"Only it's golden, not orange," I pointed out.

"Missy Violet would be so proud of you," Mama said as she watched me wrap the goldenseal up in a kitchen towel we had brought. But when we got home and Mama was telling everybody how good I was at gathering roots and herbs, I remembered something that made me feel as dumb as a rock.

"Mama!" I whispered.

"What's the matter?" Mama asked.

"I forgot something real important."

"What?"

"The roots have to be dried and ground up."

"All right," Mama said.

"But it takes weeks for them dry," I said, "and Mary Lee needs the medicine right away."

"Oh, that is a fly in the buttermilk," Mama said. "But you still know your beans, honey. You remembered that the roots have to be dried. That's very good."

"But what about Mary Lee?" I asked.

"Well, she'll just have to wait. You meant well, baby."

"I know," I said. "I can go over to Missy Violet's and go in her glass cabinet and get some goldenseal that's already made into tea and take it to Mary Lee."

"Now, you can't go in Missy Violet's house while she's away," Mama said.

"But Savannah or one of the boys goes down there every day to feed Duke and the cow."

"I don't care. You can't go trespassin' inside someone's house while she's away. Now, that's that!" Mama pressed her lips together tight like the clasp on a change purse, and I knew she meant what she said.

That afternoon Charles asked if he could borrow one of my lead pencils so he could do his homework, and that gave me an idea. "Maybe I could borrow some golden-seal tea from one of Missy Violet's nervous patients." But who? Miss Roula? No, Miss Roula took boneset tonic for the tired blood. Miss Sarah Bright? No, Miss Bright took a little blackberry wine. Then it came to me like a bright ray of sunshine: Miss Petty! Miss Petty was a little sliver of a lady who played the piano at church. A spinster lady who fluttered like a hummingbird every time someone spoke to her. Missy Violet always took her skullcap and pennyroyal and goldenseal for her nerves. Maybe she still had some.

But Miss Petty kept to herself and didn't like children. Especially since the time Missy Violet sent me over to her house with some tea and Charles followed me over there and acted the fool. He got up under Miss Petty's window and made his voice go up real high and hollered, "Miz Pity, Miz Pity Pity!"

Miss Petty came to the window and looked out. When she saw Charles, her eyes got as big as saucers and she started to scream. Miss Petty is scared to death of men and boys. She didn't even see me. I tried to tell her it was me with her tea, but Charles in his devilment kept squallin', "Miz Pity, Miz Pity!" and the poor lady got so nervous and confused, she ran straight through the house and out the back door! So Missy Violet had to deliver the tea herself. Now when Miss Petty sees me or Charles at church, she starts to shake all over.

I don't know how to ask Miss Petty for her tea now. How am I going to help poor Mary Lee?

I want to write and tell Missy Violet all about Mary Lee, but Mama would kill me. She'd say I was getting in grown folks' business. I know Mama will tell Missy Violet all about it when she comes home.

Mama and Miss Petty

I told Arma Jean about Mary Lee. She said she would go with me to see Miss Petty. We didn't let Charles know about our plan. But Mama found out about it and told Arma Jean and me, "Leave that poor soul alone!" She said the safe thing to do would be to let her ask Miss Petty. But will she listen to Mama?

Mama approached Miss Petty at church one Sunday. Arma Jean and I were watching as Mama walked up to the piano. Miss Petty flinched when she heard Mama behind her. "Good mornin', Merlene. How you this fine Sunday mornin'?" Mama said in a real easy voice, and Miss Petty looked up at Mama over the top of her spectacles.

"Merlene? She don't look like a Merlene," Arma Jean whispered.

"I think that's a nice name," I whispered back to Arma Jean.

"Yeah, but Merlene? She look more like a Lula or an Oola or somethin'," Arma Jean said a little loud, and Mama turned around and gave us a hard look.

"How do!" Miss Petty answered, and snatched a handkerchief out of her pocketbook and started polishing the piano keys.

"Merlene," Mama went on, "I'm startin' a quilt and I'd like for somebody to work on it with me. I thought about you because I hear you do some of the finest stitchin' in town. Would you be good enough to work on it with me? I'm startin' it tomorrow afternoon."

Miss Petty kept her head down, but when she looked up her eyes had water in them and said, "I'd be much obliged, Lena."

Miss Petty and Mama sewed up a storm that Monday afternoon, and by the time I got home from school,

Mama had the goldenseal tea for Mary Lee. Good work, Mama!

Not only that, but Mama said Miss Petty was one of the best sewers she's ever seen. "Stitches straight as arrows just like a sewin' machine. Sixteen stitches to the inch!" Mama said. And coming from Mama that's a good word, because Mama is one of the best seamstresses in the county. Mama said when she asked Miss Petty about the tea, she said she'd be "more than happy to share with Mary Lee."

Mama said Charles came home from school while Miss Petty was still at the house. Mama and I both believe he meant to get home early so he could frighten Miss Petty. That's why he didn't wait to walk home from school with the rest of us. Mama said Charles came in with an impish look on his face. She said poor Miss Petty's hands began to shake as soon as Charles walked through the door.

Mama fixed Charles good, though. She said she did her finger for Charles to come over to her and she whispered in his ear, "If you upset Miss Petty, I'll break you down into five dollars' worth of change!" And Charles skulked on out of the room with a long face. Good for Mama! I think Mama will be a nice friend for Miss Petty.

Mama and I went by to see Mary Lee every day for a week, and sure enough, she began to feel better after drinking the tea. I was real proud of myself. This was the second time I had looked after somebody while Missy Violet was away. Maybe someday I *could* make a good midwife.

Mama Gets a Letter
from Missy Violet

November 7, 1929

Dear Lena,

I hope this letter finds you all in the Lord's
care. Brother is improving every day and we
are grateful for God's mercy. How is James's
foot? Be sure to give him my regards and tell
him I appreciate him and the children looking
after Duke and the cow for me. If Brother keeps
improving, I hope to be home by New Year's.

How is that sweet baby Cleo? I'm working on
a sweater dress for her while I'm here in Florida.

Brother usually goes to bed early and I sit and knit while he sleeps.

How is Savannah? Is she keeping company yet? My heart goes out to you and James. I know you have your hands full with so many children in the flower of their youth. I keep you in my prayers always.

Lena, I want you to do something for me. Please go visit little Maggie Dockery and see if she is doing her hand calisthenics. Take Viney with you — she will know what to do. And if you can, please go by and see little Bennie Sattifield and his mother. Let me know how they are coming along.

I will be much obliged if you will see to this for me. And if you happen to see Miss Roula, give her a hug for me. Give everybody at church my regards and give Viney and Charles a hug and a kiss. They are my two sugar lumps. May God bless you and yours.

In Christian love,

Viola McCrae

November 16, 1929

Dear Missy Violet,

So good to hear from you. Things are not the same with you away. James and the children are fine. His foot finally got better. For a while I thought my husband was going to be crippled for life. Thank the Lord you sent word for him to stay off it and he listened. And for Viney doing all the things you had taught her.

Don't worry, I will do what you asked. Viney and I will go see little Maggie Dockery and little Bennie Sattifield. I saw little Bennie in town with Miss Mintzy, that old lady who takes care of him while his mother and father go to work. When anybody talks to her she holds on to that little sack she wears tied around her neck. It's just some grass and twigs tied up in some muslin, but she think its got some kind of magic in it.

You should see Bennie. He is a great big strong baby. Twice as big as Cleo. I don't know how Miss Mintzy handles him—she's all bent over and got the rheumatis in her hands. I'm surprised Bennie hasn't snatched that amulet from around her neck.

Yes, ma'am, Savannah is keeping company. She is seeing Solomon Trueheart. You know, that part-Indian boy. They will be graduating in May. James don't like it, though—he favors Lorendo Smith. He and Lorendo fixed it so Savannah would catch Solomon with that fast gal, Windrella Rodgers. Savannah nearly died when she saw the two of them together—I had to step in and tell her about James and Lorendo's little trick. James don't know I told. He doesn't even know I know. Now he just thinks it's the Lord's will that Savannah and Solomon got together.

The boys are fine, except for Claude Thomas. You know he's my peculiar child. I have not told anybody about this, but I may have to send him away. He says he's going to kill one of the Klan. Lord have mercy! I think what set him off was what happened to Charles and Viney a little while ago when they went fishing up on the river.

Even after the children told him about the little white boy who saved them, he still felt the same way. He says he's going to get a shotgun and kill the first white person he sees, and you know, Missy Violet, he's always going off by himself. Half the time I don't know where he is. I'm so worried about him.

One day, Antonio Rose said to me, "Mama, you know, I

been thinkin'. Claude Thomas ain't doin nothin' down in the woods but drawin' pictures of animals and birds and things." And, Missy Violet, he can draw a picture of anything. The boy really is gifted in that way.

But he doesn't have any friends—not one. Everybody should have at least one friend. Antonio Rose says the pictures are his friends. You know Antonio Rose, always figuring things out. And I do declare, Missy Violet, what Antonio Rose said did set my mind at ease for a while.

Pray for us. Pray for our boy to have patience to wait on the Lord to make things right for the colored people. I didn't mean to burden you with my problems, I know you have your own worries. But the Bible says, "The fervent prayer of the righteous availeth much."

Faithfully yours,

Lena Windbush

LITTLE BENNIE AND LITTLE MAGGIE

November 19, 1929

Dear Missy Violet,

I am writing this letter for Mama. She wanted to write it herself, but I begged her to let me write it for her so I could get to use my new green writing paper I won in the essay contest. She wants you to know that the last time Papa and the boys went down to your house to lay down straw for the cow and to feed the dog, Mama and I went by Miss Roula's house. But her daughter had already closed up the house and taken Miss Roula up north. So we went to see little Bennie Sattifield and his mama.

Little Bennie is special because he is the first baby I helped bring into the world. He is all plump and rosy now—not like the first time I saw him. Back then he was all wrinkly and red and squalling his head off! Now he laughs and coos and tries to catch things in the air with his little dimpled hands. I asked Missus Sattifield if I could hold him and she sat him on my lap. He was so heavy. I think he is heavier than my baby sister, Cleo, though Cleo is older.

It felt good holding little Bennie, and that big wide grin that hides inside of me came out and spread across my face. Little Bennie kept looking up at me with his pretty round eyes. I wondered if he remembered me. I wondered if he was grateful that I had held him after he was born. Then he hauled off and clocked me in the nose! I could taste blood in my mouth. Missus Sattifield rushed over and took little Bennie, and Mama gave me a handkerchief to wipe my nose with. It felt like my two front teeth were loose.

Miss Sattifield said, "I'm so sorry, child. He a little slaphappy." Then she said to the baby, "Little Bennie, that wasn't nice. Why you hit Viney? She's your friend." But little Bennie just said, "Gugh!"

By the time we got to Missus Dockery's house the bleeding had stopped and my two front teeth were not loose. Little Maggie was in the yard playing when we walked up. When she saw us she ran into the house. Her mama came through the screen door and invited us to sit down on the porch. Mama and Missus Dockery chitchatted for a while. Then Mama told Missus Dockery about your letter, that you were concerned about Maggie's hands.

Missus Dockery called Maggie over and told her to show me and Mama her hands. The little girl was shamefaced at first and hid her hands behind her back. So I said, "Come here, Maggie. I want to show you something." When she came over I balled up my fists and held them up.

"Did you know that all babies are born with their hands balled into fists like this? But they are supposed to open up in a few months. See, like this." I spread my fingers. Maggie looked at my hands then looked at her own. "Missy Violet told me that sometimes a baby's hands won't open up on their own so you got to help them. You got to let your mama pull them every day, and you got to sleep with them under your head or under your pillow. You remember how Missy Violet showed you?" And Maggie nodded her head.

"Now show me what you're going to do," I said, and Maggie pressed her little crooked hands together like in prayer, then she rested them under her cheek like they were a pillow. "That's right, Maggie!" I said, and gave her a hug like you do when you talk to her. That felt good, like when I was holding little Bennie, only Maggie didn't punch me in the nose.

So don't worry about Maggie and little Bennie—they are doing fine. Mama said we would go back and visit them in a few weeks if you were not home by then. She says to give your brother our regards and to tell you all the family is well.

From your best helper girl,

Viney

Mister Som Grit
and the Rausy Brothers

November 23, 1929
Dear Missy Violet,

There was a lot of excitement at the church a few Sundays ago. Maybe you already heard about it because everybody is talking about it, saying it was a sign, on account of what happened a few days after. Those crazy Rausy Brothers showed up at church service! All the older folk said never since there was an African Methodist Episcopal Church in Richmond County had a Rausy stepped foot in a church! But there they were—both of them, looking like two train wrecks.

Some folks think they ran out of food back there in the woods and came down to the church to find something to eat. But Reverend Mims believes the Lord sent them to get saved because Pax, the one with the funny-shaped head, went to the Moanin' Bench and got religion. Bledsoe didn't go up, but he did clap his hands and pat his foot when Savior Brown sang "Oh, Happy Day." But later, he started that herky-jerky laugh of his and kept it up right through Reverend Mims's sermon. After that, he had to be escorted out of the church for picking at some of the sisters.

Next thing you know, Mister Som Grit jumps up and starts testifying. Everybody was surprised because he's a "Baptist born, Baptist bred, and when I die, I'll be a Baptist dead" Baptist. Some of the folks think he came over to the Methodist to find a wife. They say he can't get a wife

over at the Baptist church because the
women there know him too well.

Arma Jean said she heard the preacher's
wife tell one of the ladies on the Usher
Board that she didn't understand why Mister
Som Grit come over to the Methodists.
She said "the pickin's are slim" at the
Methodist church because "most of the
women Mister Grit's age are settled widow
ladies who don't want to be bothered with
no husbands no more" and the rest are "old
maids who are afraid of men."

Arma Jean had an idea. She thinks Miss
Petty should get with Mister Som Grit.
She thinks Miss Petty secretly wants to
be a married lady, and she thinks she knows
how to get Mister Som Grit and Miss
Petty together. That girl is a genius!

But something happened a few days later
that made us forget about Mister Som
Grit and Miss Petty. One of the Rausy
Brothers passed away. The one named Pax,
with the funny-shaped head, just up and

died. His brother, Bledsoe, stayed in the house with him for three days before he told anybody he was dead. He finally went to Reverend Mims and Reverend Mims sent Mister Brownlee out there to get the body.

It was real nice the way everybody pitched in to help. Mama said it was the Christian thing to do. Mama and Miss Petty put together a dark suit for Pax Rausy, and the undertaker donated a pine box. The Goodwill Workers cooked food, and the Usher Board brought flowers. On the day of the funeral the church was packed. Mama said some of those folks just came there "to see."

Some of the menfolk got Bledsoe all cleaned and shaved and gussied up for his brother's funeral, and he didn't look half bad, except when he opened his mouth and showed those fangs he got for teeth.

Pax Rausy was buried in the church graveyard thanks to Reverend Mims. He says there will be a place for Bledsoe, too, because the brothers were feeble-minded and had no kin.

I have to close now. Tomorrow is a school day.

Yours truly,

Viney

Papa's Dilemma

Papa is worried about his job at Liggett and Meyers Tobacco Company, where he makes and cuts cigarettes. They laid off about half of their workers a few weeks ago, most of them colored. Papa expects to be laid off any day now. "Guess I'll be turnin' in my blue uniform soon," he keeps mumbling as he walks around the house. Lately he's been talking about moving north. Every evening at the supper table Papa starts talking about going to Chicago or New York City or New Jersey. My heart quivers like a fiddle bow every time we sit down to eat, because I know Mama and Papa are going to argue about "going up north."

Savannah and Mama and I think it is a bad idea to move up north, but Papa and the boys think it's the best idea Papa ever had. Especially Antonio Rose, my youngest brother. He's the one who likes to stick up under Papa all the time, going along with anything Papa says. He's even named after Papa's mama, Rose Velvet, who was standing at the foot of the bed when he was being born, and died in her sleep that night.

James Clyde, my oldest brother, said he was going to sell Brown Bisquit, the beautiful chestnut horse Grandpapa gave him, so he could buy a Buick and drive Papa all the way up to Chicago, where Papa's cousin Essex lives. Roosevelt, my brother next to James Clyde, keeps talking about the fine clothes he's going to buy when he gets up north. Savannah said, "Roosevelt, I declare, you care more about clothes than you do about the Lord," and everybody laughed.

"And he uses Mama's smoothin' iron more than Mama does on them," I said, and even Roosevelt had to laugh, because it was true. Mama never had to tell him to hang up his clothes or brush off his shoes. Sometimes he would even pay somebody to iron for him. He's real handsome and dudish, but not biggety. All the girls are crazy about him.

Claude Thomas, my peculiar brother, says he can't wait to go up north with Papa so he won't have to miss the beginning of school every year to pick cotton. Usually, he just sits quietly whenever they get to talking about going north. He's the one Mama worries about all the time, because he's kind of moody and surly and don't know how to stay in his place with the white folk.

Getting back to Papa, one evening at the supper table he cleared his throat and said in a friendly voice, "I hear Joe Gladney done moved up to New Jersey and got hisself a good-payin' job at an automobile factory."

"We goin' too, Papa?" Antonio squawked. But before Papa could say a word, Mama said, "Eat your supper, Antonio Rose." Then she turned to Papa. "I thought we had already buried that bone, James?" And there was a little ice in her voice when she said it.

"Now, don't go gettin' your teeth on edge, Lena," Papa shot back at Mama. "It's not like I'm askin' you to go to East Jublipp or someplace. We wouldn't be the first family that got up and moved north — lotta folks doin' it.

And if I had had my way, we would have gone ten years ago!" Papa sounded angry.

"You mean you already forgot all the trouble you had the last time you tried goin' up north?" Mama asked. "Why, you almost went to jail!"

"Papa almost went to jail!" Savannah and I both squealed at the same time.

"Yes. Him and a lot of other colored men," Mama answered, and commenced telling us about the time two labor agents from Detroit came down to recruit colored men for work in the steel mills up north. Mama said a bunch of colored men who had just signed up with the agents were waiting at the train depot when the sheriff came and locked them all up, white labor agents and all. "Your papa almost went to jail too," Mama said. "But when Sheriff Rainey couldn't find a train ticket on him or a copy of the *Chicago Defender,* he let him go home."

"What's the *Chicago Defender?*" Antonio asked, and James Clyde told him it was a northern newspaper that told colored people they should come north for a better life. Mama said Papa's cousin Essex sent him a copy every month. She said she warned Papa that something bad was going to happen if he didn't stop reading that northern newspaper. She said she'd decided that the next copy that came into the house would go right into the fire!

Papa looked like he had a bad taste in his mouth while Mama was talking. "That was a bad year, Lena," he said. "A heap of colored folks migrated north that year. They had to. The boll weevils ruined all the cotton crops, and storms and floods ruined the rest. Plantation workers like me couldn't get no work. What was I supposed to do?"

Mama acted like she hadn't heard a word Papa said. "James," she said, "all those folks who go up north come back down here garnished with diamonds and pearls and putting on fancy airs. Tellin' us now 'swell' it is in New York City and Chicago and New Jersey—they're not tellin' the truth! Esther Green's been writin' to me ever since she went up there to live, and she tells me how hard it is to make ends meet. How cold it is. And how colored folks got to pay almost three times as much rent as white folks."

Papa put on a stubborn face. "I still want to go," he growled. "I'm tired of bowin' and scrapin' and callin' the foreman 'boss' and 'captain.' I'm tired of my children havin' to stay home from school to tend cotton. Lord knows, all I want is a chance to make a better life for my family!" Papa said.

When Papa said those words, Mama's face changed, and I could tell she was sorry she had fussed at him. She said, "Eat your supper, James, before you get one of your sick headaches. We can talk about this later." But this time her voice was sweet and mild.

MISSUS DAISY MONROE

November 28, 1929
Dear Missy Violet,

  Do you know Missus Daisy Monroe?
Mama really admires Missus Monroe because
she is a fine seamstress and has her own
dressmaking business in Durham, North
Carolina. One day while Mama and I were at
the general store, we met Missus Monroe
and right away Mama began to complain to
Missus Monroe about Papa pining to go up
north. "He got a bad case of the itchin'

foot," Mama told her. Missus Monroe didn't seem surprised at all. "That's nothing to be upset about, Lena. Folks go up north all the time," she said. "People lookin' for decent work. A fine seamstress like yourself could get plenty of piecework in a blouse or dress factory up there," she told Mama.

"I was there myself in nineteen twenty-five," Missus Monroe said, and Mama's mouth flew open like a baby bird's. "I stayed a whole year, had my own customers and everything," she told Mama. She said she would have stayed longer but her mother took sick and she had to come back home to wait on her.

"Is that so?" Mama said.

"My daughter is up in Chicago right now, in nursing school," Missus Monroe told Mama, and smiled real proud. "She'll be a hospital nurse when she gets through." When Missus Monroe said "nursing school," my ears began to tingle, and I forgot my manners and butt in to Mama and Missus Monroe's conversation.

"You mean they have a nursing school for colored girls up north?" I squawked, and Mama gave me a hard look for speaking out of turn. But Missus Monroe laughed and said, "Why, yes, child. It's called the Provident Hospital Training School, and it's owned and run by colored."

"Well, for goodness' sakes!" I said. And Mama and Missus Monroe couldn't help but laugh. I didn't know what else to say. A school for colored nurses—imagine that! A school owned and run by colored people! Miss Battle was right: Colored people are doing fine things in all the trades every day now. Going up north didn't sound so bad after all.

After Missus Monroe talked to Mama, Mama got over being mad at Papa for wanting to go up north. I guess she decided it wasn't the worst thing in the world, because more than anything else, Mama just wants Papa to be happy.

But I still don't want to leave my friends and family. Not only that, but who would help you "catch babies" if I went away? I have an idea. Maybe Papa will let me come back every summer, and I'm sure he and Mama will let Arma Jean come up for a visit once in a while. Now I feel better about going, especially when I think about getting a vacation from Charles.

Yours truly,

Viney

So Much to Talk About
When I Get Home

December 4, 1929

Dear Viney,

I hope this letter finds you and the family well. I had hoped to be home by the holidays, but Brother still needs me. I have been reading all of your letters. Sometimes I read them more than once when I start to miss you all. You are very watchful and alert to everything that is going on around you. That is a good quality. And you really care about others. That is one of the things I love about you.

I want to thank you and your mother for

going to see about Little Bennie and little Maggie Dockery for me. I'm happy you found them doing well. I knew that Little Bennie was going to be a little devil by the way he jumped into the world! Bless his heart.

Now, little Maggie Dockery is very shy. You will have to visit her often to make sure she does her calisthenics. Sometimes take her a small gift, a used toy that she can hold in her hands to encourage her, and give her mother my love.

I was very sorry to hear about one of the Rausy brothers passing away. It was kind of Reverend Mims and the church members to do what they did.

You asked me if I knew Missus Daisy Monroe: I know of her but I don't know her personally. I have heard about her fine sewing. I didn't know she had a daughter in nursing school up north. That is wonderful! Like I always say, the world is changing all the time. I think you would make a fine nurse, Viney. Seems like we have a great deal to talk about when I get home. We will have to sit by the fire and talk for a long, long while.

Is your daddy still excited about going north? Lots of people are doing it. Going north has its good points and its bad points, but chances of getting a good education probably are better in the North. I'd like to know more about the nursing schools up there. Yes, we have a lot to talk about.

How is school? When will you get your report card? Let me know how your grades are. Give Charles my love and kiss Cleo for me. Give the whole family my regards. Brother sends his regards too.

Yours very truly,
Missy Violet

Cousin Essex

December 12, 1929
Dear Missy Violet,

   After we all got used to the idea of
moving north, Papa got a letter from his
cousin Essex who lives in Chicago. Papa read
the letter at the supper table.

   "Hello, James," it began.

   I hope this letter finds you and Lena and
the children in God's care. Guess you are
wondering what took me so long to answer
the last letter you wrote me, asking about

places to stay in Chicago while you look for work. The reason is that things are very bad up here now. You all probably already heard that we are in a depression. Back in October, most of the rich white folks up here lost all their money in the stock market crash, and that brought everybody down a peg or two.

A lot of factories had to close down, and a lot of wealthy families had to let their cooks and maids and chauffeurs go. Colored people are having rent parties to help pay the rent. Colored and white alike are standing in soup lines, and some are looking through garbage cans for scraps of food to feed their families and for wood to keep them warm.

People are freezing to death. PEOPLE ARE FREEZING TO DEATH. We are all having a hard time up here. Some folks may have to go on relief.

I lost my good job at the shipyard, but by the Lord's grace, I got a job at a colored funeral home. It's only two days a week. And Sadie's job at the laundry been cut down to one day. Thank the Lord for folks dyin'. Things are real hard, cousin, so I can't invite you to come stay with us right now. You all stay down home where you can at least grow something to eat and keep a roof over your heads and keep warm. Sadie cry all the time now, say we should come back home. I don't know, have to see how things turn out up here. Please keep us in your prayers.

    Your cousin,

    Essex Windbush

    When Papa finished reading the letter, his face looked like a road map, with all the lines and veins. A worried look came over Mama's face, too, but she didn't say a word. Papa laid the letter down on the table and walked out of the room. We sure did feel sorry for our Papa. We were all disappointed too.

Papa didn't have much to say to anyone for the next week or two. But Mama never said "I told you so." She tried to humor Papa and fixed all his favorite foods. Finally, he came around and started talking again, and we were all glad to have our old Papa back. Not long after that he got a job at Mister J. A. McAulay's textile mill as a cleaning man. It didn't work out too bad, because Papa could bring home all the scraps he wanted. And he brought home some beautiful materials for Mama and Savannah. I wish he could get a job in an ice cream factory.

From your best helper girl,

Viney

A Wedding

December 19, 1929
Dear Missy Violet,

Surprise, surprise! Mister Som Grit married Miss Petty. Folks can't stop talking about it. Arma Jean is the only one *not* surprised because she's the one who said "Miss Petty need to marry Mister Som Grit" in the first place.

It happened so fast that some of the ladies at the church had to scare up a wedding. They said a lady Miss Petty's age deserved a dignified wedding. So the ladies on the Usher Board set up some long tables on the church grounds, and the congregation brought enough food to feed a pharaoh's army.

Mama and Miss Petty and Savannah got together and made the most beautiful dress. Arma Jean said she heard Miss Petty already had a dress in her hope chest, but it was wore out from waitin' so long. But the dress she and Mama and Savannah made was all lacy with pearls and creamy white like the icing on a cake.

Arma Jean and I sat together in the front row. Miss Lutie Mae Darkchild and her sisters tried to shoo us away because they wanted those front-row seats, but Arma Jean stood up to them and they backed off. We knew they just wanted to laugh and make fun of Miss Petty when she came down the aisle because they were jealous.

Papa walked Miss Petty down the aisle. He didn't want to do it but Mama made him. Mama told Miss Petty to be sure and hold her head up high when she came down the aisle. And Mama wouldn't let her wear her spectacles. "James will guide you down the aisle," she told her. She told Miss Petty to think of herself as a princess so Mister Som Grit would be proud when he saw her. Mama and Missus Mims put a little lipstick and a little rouge and a little powder on Miss Petty, and she was almost pretty. The Darkchild sisters couldn't close their mouths, they were so shocked at how good Miss Petty looked. Everybody was shocked.

Mister Som Grit didn't look bad himself. He wore a black suit with tails, and patent leather shoes. His hair was parted down the middle and slicked back. He didn't wear his derby, thank the Lord. A Mister Willie Poe from across the river stood up with him in the church. Mister Som Grit kept wipin' his brow the whole time he was saying his vows. But after he finally got the ring on

Miss Petty's finger and "kissed the bride," they sashayed out of the church husband and wife and everybody had a fine time. I hope they are going to be happy. Somebody said Miss Nula Irish tried to trip the bride while she was coming down the aisle, but they said Papa saw her and gave her the fish eyes and she pulled her foot back in. Arma Jean and I missed that. As far as we saw, Miss Petty got down the aisle smooth as cream. I thought Charles would pull one of his pranks, but I guess he remembered what Mama told him she would do to him if he messed with Miss Petty, so he behaved himself at the wedding. Weddings are so nice.

I know Mama is going to kill me for writing this letter. She'll say I was being grown and fast, writing about grown folks' business again. But I just had to tell you about the wedding.

Yours truly,
Viney

MISTER SOM GRIT

Before the wedding, Mister Som Grit wrote Miss Petty a letter. I know because Miss Petty came over to our house and asked Mama what she should do. Then she gave Mama the letter and ran out the door. I just happened to be standing in the next room when she came. Mama read it, slipped the letter in her apron pocket, and started fixing lunch.

That afternoon Arma Jean came over and I told her what happened and she said we *had* to get that letter and read it. So when Mama took her apron off and hung it on the nail behind the door, Arma Jean and I slipped it out of her pocket and read it. It said:

Dear Miss Petty,

Let me tell you something about myself. I'm a poor widow man who lost his wife two years ago. Her name was Mary Faye and she was a good Christian woman. We had one child, born dead. We named her Elizabeth Faye. She up in heaven now. We did not have any more children.

I been askin the Lord to send me another wife. I am a lonely man. I can take good care of a wife. I got a house, some land, and my own automobile. I am retired now, but I was the buggy driver for the Rakestraw family for twenty-five years. They give me one of their automobiles so I could drive around in style after I retired. It's a big ol' shiny Packard. You most likely done seen me drivin around in it. I'd like to give you a ride in it sometimes.

I might as well tell you, cause you

bound to find out someday: I was tryin to talk to Miss Viola McCrae and
Miss Nula Irish, but they snubbed me.
So I been lookin at you for a while now.
You seems like a nice settled lady and
that's what I'm lookin for. I ain't
lookin for no fast, loose woman to run
through my money like water. I'm lookin
for a nice quiet, settled lady like
yourself. I likes it that you can play
the pianna too.

Please let me know what you think
of my letter.
Very Truly Yours,
Somilant Grit

Miss Petty came back the next day and asked Mama a zillion questions. "What should I do?" "Do you think he really likes me?" "Do you think I'm too old?" "Which house will we live in?"

"Do you want to get married?" Mama asked Miss Petty.

"Oh, yes!" Miss Petty answered. "But I never thought

anyone would ask me. I thought I was too old, and too homely," Miss Petty said.

"Phooey!" Mama said. "Does he make you feel happy?" Mama asked.

"He makes me laugh," said Miss Petty. "Not that he says funny things, but he looks kind of funny," explained Miss Petty.

"Is that so?" said Mama.

"Yes, he's like a big ol' teddy bear."

"Do that bother you?" Mama asked.

"No. He's sort of cute and helpless like a baby," Miss Petty said.

"He's got his own house and a car," Mama reminded Miss Petty.

Miss Petty started wringing her hands. "Oh dear, oh dear. I don't know the first thing about pleasing a man," she said.

Finally, Mama said in a patient voice, "Look, Merlene, the man is lonely. He needs someone to look after him. Can you do that?"

"Yes," Miss Petty said.

MISSY VIOLET COMES HOME

When Missy Violet came home after New Year's, Mama had her over for supper one evening and she told us the whole story about her poor brother. He had been a very sick man, but instead of going to a regular doctor for his ailment, he was going to an ol' snake doctor who was giving him some kind of oil to drink and rub on his body. By the time Missy Violet got there he was almost dead. She took him to a real doctor and the doctor put him in the hospital right away. He's much better now, so Missy Violet was able to come home.

Everybody wanted to sit next to Missy Violet at the dinner table that night — we were all so glad she was back!

But Mama sat her between James Clyde and Charles. That took Charles up a few buttonholes. After supper all of us children hung around, asking Missy Violet questions about Tallahassee. Even Claude Thomas remained at the table, although he doesn't care much for company. We are all hoping that Missy Violet can get him to calm down inside before he gets himself killed by the Klan. Things just seem so right when Missy Violet is here in Richmond County.

Missy Violet said that Tallahassee, Florida, was one of the most beautiful places she'd ever visited. With beaches and freshwater springs and gardens and palm trees everywhere. Charles wanted to know about the funny name "Tallahassee." Missy Violet said that her brother told her it was an Indian name that meant "old fields."

Missy Violet said there are a lot of Indians in Florida. She said they were fine-looking people who liked to dress in beautiful, colorful clothes. Many people came down to Florida just to see them and to buy things they made on the Indian reservation where they live. Missy Violet brought us some gifts from the reservation: an Indian doll for baby Cleo, some pretty glass beads for me and Savannah, a little wooden alligator for Charles. A woven basket for Mama and leather wallets for Papa and the boys. Charles wanted a wallet too, but I guess Missy Violet thought he would get himself in trouble with it. She even brought flowers and flower seeds. Tickseed. They are a favorite flower in Florida. Yellow and shaped like a sunflower around the edges, red or mahogany-colored in the center. Missy Violet says when they grow the stems are so thin, the flowers look like they are floating on air. She says lots of butterflies will come where they are. Mama can't wait to plant them.

Those were not the only gifts she brought. There was also smoked sausage that tastes better than the smoked sausage we make here in Richmond County, though I didn't think that was possible. Oranges and grapefruits. Our family hardly ever sees a grapefruit. And Missy Violet's brother sent us a recipe for Lima Bean Pot. Mmm. Missy Violet's brother was a cook at the governor's mansion before he got sick, and Missy Violet says he knows lots of good recipes.

But what I liked best was when she talked about the Seminole Indians' folk medicine. She looked right at me while she was talking. That made me feel good that she thought I was interested—and I was. She said she brought back some corn shuck tea, because the Indians say it is good for rashes. Missy Violet hopes it will help Mister Johnnie Browne's weeping eczema. If it doesn't, she can try a poultice made from witch hazel, which she also brought back. Missy Violet thinks of everyone!

Well, Charles couldn't wait to say something about Savannah and Solomon Trueheart. Savannah dropped her head and blushed when Charles let the cat out of the bag. Missy Violet asked her if that was true, if she was keeping company with Solomon Trueheart. I guess Missy Violet didn't know what else to do after the way Charles blurted it out.

"Yes'um," Savannah said in a little itty-bitty voice, and Papa started shuffling his feet underneath the table.

"You keep yourself firm like a wall, you hear?" Missy Violet said to Savannah in her "I mean business" voice. "And don't let no boy trip you up. I'll be watchin' you."

"Yes, ma'am, I will," Savannah said. Then Missy Violet turned to James Clyde, my oldest brother, and asked him when he was going to take a wife. But James Clyde said he was going to wait.

"Missy Violet, I'm tryin' to establish a small lumber business for myself before I takes a wife," he said.

"Now, that's a fine thing," Missy Violet said. "I like that, but remember to be a gentleman while you waitin'," she told him.

I think all the talk about courting and marriage made Papa nervous. He started talking about something else: Me! He told Missy Violet how I had gone into the woods with Mama and gathered goldenseal to help poor Mary Lee Williams. And how I had visited the little Dockery girl and little Bennie. "I think my girl would make a fine hospital nurse," Papa said. I never knew Papa even paid attention to those kinds of things when I did them! I think he was proud of me. I felt a big grin spread across my face. A big grin spread across Missy Violet's face too.

"Well, children, it's been a fine evening, but it's getting late and I best be getting on home," Missy Violet said, and rose from her seat. Mama, Savannah, and I walked her to the door. Missy Violet hugged us, and then she said to me, "Viney, two Saturdays from today, I want you, Arma Jean, Charles, Mister Waters's boy Cleveland, Ruby Dean, and your new friend Mister Brownlee's niece to come over for cake and lemonade. Missy Violet is going to bake the biggest coconut cake you ever did see."

I felt real special after Missy Violet left, but Charles

tried to make me feel bad. He came over and whispered in my ear, "You too dumb to be a hospital nurse." But I didn't believe him. I believe if I work real hard in school and learn to read well, and learn all I can from Missy Violet about roots and herbs and babies and people, I will be able to go to that nursing school up in Chicago some-day. Maybe they even have a nursing school I could go to down in Tallahassee, Florida.

"The world is changing all the time," Missy Violet al-ways says.